Billy let Colonel ~~a little more.~~
"You know we're all related but nobody knows how, right?"

"Teacher said something once in school, I recollect," Billy answered, a little cloudy from the Lightnin' he'd been drinking. "But what it was, exactly . . ."

"We're a mighty proud and fiercely loyal bunch, Billy my boy. Started out that way years ago—oh, long before that chickenshit Chinee war began. Maybe fifty years ago? The old auto and motorbike clubs an' clans stuck together. Nobody was blood kin to anybody else. But once the clans started livin' on the road and travelin' in groups, like with like, things changed. Not having much education . . . to keep proper records, when a couple got hitched, their children remembers, but their grandchildren didn't. And when some little bastard needed a name, it was took from the great American roadside we know and love almost better'n we love that old time religion."

Meet These Americans of Tomorrow:
The Peels, Rallyes, Rollbars and
Afterburners—the generations

ON

WHEELS

Also by John Jakes

Six-Gun Planet
The Asylum World

published by
WARNER BOOKS

ON WHEELS

John Jakes

WARNER BOOKS

A Warner Communications Company

Warner Books are
distributed in the
United Kingdom by

NEW ENGLISH LIBRARY

WARNER BOOKS EDITION

Copyright © 1973 by John Jakes
Member, Science Fiction Writers of America
All rights reserved

ISBN 0-446-89932-1

Cover art by David Plourde

Warner Books, Inc., 75 Rockefeller Plaza, New York, N.Y. 10019

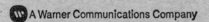A Warner Communications Company

Printed in Canada.

Not associated with Warner Press, Inc., of Anderson, Indiana

First Printing: May, 1973

Reissued: October, 1978

10 9 8 7 6 5 4 3

For my wife,

who has seen me through.

And all the while, standing by in full Shy, in alumicron suits—there is Detroit, hardly able to believe itself what it has discovered, a breed of good old boys from the fastnesses of the Appalachian hills and flats—a handful from this rare breed—who have given Detroit . . . speed . . . and the industry can present it to a whole generation as . . . yours.

—Tom Wolfe,
THE LAST AMERICAN HERO IS
JUNIOR JOHNSON. YES!

ON WHEELS

i / Low Gear

"Life, liberty, and the pursuit of mileage."

—FOLK SAYING

He was drifting along at 85 mph, just drifting, under the fat Nevada moon that iced the distant mountains, when the radiophone blinked.

The tiny red dashlight went on and off, on and off, slowly, like an injured eye. Billy stared at the spot of color a minute, his mouth tightening up and his mind cooling and coiling. God damn that light. God damn it because there weren't many moments like this in a man's life: alone, quiet, in the bucket of a mother with a big i.c. underhood engine bubbling and muttering and blowing out a thin blueness from the dual exhausts.

He wore neither crash helmet nor belts and, because the Twister was old, an authentic machine from the early '80s when his father had been but a young man, there was a sense of challenge in him hard to express but beautiful to feel: here it was just him, just Billy and lightly padded instrument board and shatterable glass and easy-crinkling hoodmetal between him and the eight empty westbound lanes washed by the moon as they rose toward the ten levels of the Calneva Superstack maybe twenty miles ahead, a concrete temple, a lovely thing, set in a notch of a pass in the mountain.

The red light glowed, went out. Glowed, went out. Billy slapped a control, then dialled too far:

"—the President has announced the lightest casualties thus far in the probing activity in the environs of Peking. The White House said there is no truth to the rumor that the 705th Airpack Infantry has belted in to reinforce the—"

Swearing, Billy fiddled till he got the right wavelength, the intercar.

13

"Somebody want something?"

"Billy?"

"Yeh, Jobe?"

"You keeping watch out behind?"

He hadn't been, but he said, "Sure." He explored the rearvision mirror quickly. Where there had been but two sets of headlamps a while ago, he now saw several; too many to count.

His second cousin, Jobe Spoiler, two years his junior, chose to let the obvious lie pass. "They come on at the last interchange," he said. "Don't think it was anything but chance. Still, they're pulling up quick."

"Recognize them?"

"Ramps."

Even though there was plenty of cool November night air roaring in through the Twister's open windows, Billy's upper lip grew wet. "They driving mothers, Jobe?"

A second voice, from the second set of headlamps closest behind, came on the link: the lugubrious, always cheering gravel-rasp of old Tal, Colonel Tal, Colonel Talmadge Spoiler, Esq., a hard charger despite his advancing years. Tal was honored in the clan because he'd completed twelve grades of education, and also because nobody knew precisely how he was related to any of them; thus it was presumed that Colonel Tal might be a key, very important, relative of each and every Spoiler, and he was treated accordingly. Colonel Tal answered, "You know them Ramps are too chickenshit to risk an arrest by ever pushin' a mother."

"They're driving their regular turbines," Jobe chimed in. "Oh-oh. There goes the first one past me—"

"Appears like he's heading up your way, Billy boy," said Tal.

"I caught a flash," said Jobe. "I think it's big Lee himself."

"There go the rest of 'em," said Tal. "Two, three—four. I don't recognize a one."

"Except Lee," said Jobe, not happily.

"Yes, right," said Colonel Tal.

Gearing down, sliding through a long banked curve

14

where the eight westbound lanes angled left, and higher, toward the Calneva Superstack, Billy examined the rear mirror again. Suddenly headlights over in one of the eight lanes going the opposite way blinded him. His bowels tightened.

The mammoth turbine van passed, heading into the east on its dozen oversize tires. Commercial vehicle; not a clan hauler. For an instant he'd known the tickle of fear that was part of driving a mother, his own gawdy orange Twister, long after most of the rest of the clan members had gone to sleep in the big lumbering communal vans. There was always the possibility of being hauled in by the Federal Highway Patrol, though not usually this late at night, only a couple of hours before morning; and not usually this far out in Nevada with the finally cooling desert rushing by blank and empty under the piers of the sixteen concrete lanes that headed to the mountains and the Calneva Superstack.

"Chickenshit," Tal said loudly suddenly. Billy flicked eyes to the mirror, saw Tal's mother yaw, veer off to the side one, two, three lanes, nearly impacting the right guardrail before the Colonel corrected. "Those Ramps ain't got an ounce of principle in their bodies."

Billy's eyes got edgy. "He swipe you?"

"Tried. I'm fine, Appears it's you they want. Bad luck you takin' point for our little cruise tonight."

"Never mind," Billy returned, "I've tangled with that Lee before."

"Never raced him, have you?" Jobe said, sounding worried.

"No, never raced him," Billy admitted. "Mostly at clan parties."

Which, on reflection, had never been much fun with any of the Ramps in attendance.

Billy concentrated on the four sets of four headlamps coming up fast—he was down to 80 mph in one of the two middle lanes of the eight, waiting to see their pleasure and humming the theme of *The Old Rugged Cross* while he waited.

The clans basically trusted each other's essential honor. No communal vans were ever locked—ever. But some clans just naturally got on together especially well, like the Spoilers and the Cloverleafs, while some were so ornery and high-mouthed, nobody cared for them—and the Ramps classified there.

Oh, everyone was always cordial at festive occasions when all the larger vehicles were locked together and rolling alongside. But there was never all-out friendliness toward the Ramps, simply because they most generally looked for trouble. Not sport; trouble. They were always bragging about their reputed blood connection with the Hardchargers, including the terrible, probably legendary demon driver, Big Daddy.

The first of the Ramp turbines pulled up alongside on his left. It was a personal two-seater, the kind a Ramp man and wife would travel in when away from the clan vehicles and out for an evening's festivity. The Ramps favored low, nasty, unadorned turbines with oversize blowholes at the back end and dark metalflake tones for the paint. If this Ramp machine streaking alongside was anything other than black, Billy couldn't tell. He concentrated on steering; the power steering plant in his mother wasn't of the best, being antique, and had to be constantly corrected.

That made this current situation ticklish: the Ramp turbine was edging in, edging in, running nearly hub to hub, so close that there couldn't be a hand's width between the caps. Billy licked his upper lip and kept his head more or less straight front. He wouldn't give the other driver any satisfaction at all. But Billy's eyes moved.

The other driver, the Ramp point man, was in fact Lee. His adenoidal voice came across the radiophone connection, barely audible above the mutter of Billy's engine and the turbine powerplant, "Why, that looks like Billy Spoiler over yonder."

"Believe it is," he said. "That you, Lee?"

"Nobody else. You boys breaking the law again?"

"Guess you could call it that."

"Guess! Hell, Billy, any kid who has to get a cheap thrill driving a gasoline engine isn't doing anything else."

"Listen, it's hard work driving a mother," Billy replied. "It's hard to do what I'm doing right now."

"What you doing, Billy?"

"Holding her steady instead of shoving over and bouncing you off the road."

Lee Ramp's laugh was flat and mean. "You Spoilers are just full of promises. But when it comes to performance—" He said an obscene word with good humor. Or so it sounded.

A pause. The turbine whined. The Twister muttered. Swooping, the eight lanes graded upward more sharply: now the Calneva Superstack couldn't be more than ten miles away, its superhighway radials jutting off from all levels to disappear into tunnels heading through the mountains west, north, and south. Blue lights like ghostly balls floated at the perimeter of every level of the Superstack, which was a glorious big version of the five-level L.A. Stack of decades ago.

Finally Billy said, "What are you boys doing in this part of the woods?"

"Oh, just running and funning some, Billy."

"Thought the Ramps were cruising up in Minnesota."

"You heard the wrong gossip. Listen, this is a lucky thing, us just bumping into you this way. I've got three of my best bunch along tonight." He mentioned three Ramp names, none of which Billy caught because he was suddenly intent on a flare of light on his right: a set of lamps coming up at top speed along a merge-in feeder that would intersect the main lanes in another mile.

Federal? Or just a stopper machine? His whole system was alert, his whole body relating to his mother, to every jounce of the rough old springs and shocks, every instant of hum of the big wide belts he carried on the wheels. The stoppers were far worse than the threat of Ramps; the Ramps at least were competent drivers, clan people, road people. But the unexpected interference of some numbskull from off the highway—some popheaded kid on a high who was accustomed to starting and stopping but unaccustomed to a moonlight run on the California-Nevada border—that was bad news.

Billy kept watching the in-boring lights on the right. "Lucky how, Lee?"

"Why, I was gonna propose a little action."

"Such as?"

Lee Ramp's laugh had that edge again. "Through the Superstack flat out."

"The lanes narrow down in there. To four."

"Why, that's right, and there's seven of us. Ought to be a real sport. Or maybe not, being as how those mothers of yours don't keep up so well—"

"I heard that," came Jobe's voice. Jobe had pulled up tight behind Billy, was riding his right rear fender. "We can match you mile for mile. We can match ole Ramps anytime."

Colonel Tal cleared his throat along the connection. "Jobe, you let Billy decide it, he's point man tonight. He'll—" A hair-raising howl of fiberglass wide belts, a clink-*spang* of old metal, and Billy caught a spew of smoke in the mirror. Colonel Tal veered back to the safe side of his lane. The smoke stopped billowing from under his tires. Tal said, "Lee Ramp?"

"Right here, old buddy."

"You tell these snotmouths you're running with that if they swipe me once more before we figure out what sort of sport we aim to have, I'll blister them off with a bagful of dirty tricks and run their tailpipes up their tailbones. You got that now?"

"I got that," Lee chuckled. "Werty, was that you?"

"The ole futz was gettin' too close," said a new voice along the link.

"You ease off till we decide whether we're going to run the Superstack, Werty."

"I don't take the kind of language that ole futz—"

"Werty, I said you ease off."

Billy glanced left for a fraction, through his open window and Lee Ramp's closed one. As they ran hub to hub with just that sliver of airspace between, he saw Ramp's face by the dashlights. Thin. Scrawny, even. He remembered how poor in color Lee Ramp had looked that last time they quarrelled. It had been at a clan get-together. A quarrel in fun, but with nastiness under the crust. They argued over who had claim on the last hot cup of ginger punch left on the table, as Billy recalled.

He despised Lee Ramp even though he could admit

the skinny man had a certain kind of doomed good looks that made some girls crazy about him. Also, Lee was a keen, competent driver despite the fact that he lacked the balls to own and operate an illegal internal combustion job on moonlight runs like this.

Like a special effect hurtling at the audience in some telly flicker, a big over-the-lanes sign zoomed up toward Billy's windshield, glaring in sparkly intensity in the headlamps:

CALNEVA SUPERSTACK LEVELS 1 — 3
RIGHT LANES ONLY
8 MILES

Sadness tugged at Billy. This peaceful, beautiful night-run had been spoiled by encountering the Ramps. There just weren't many times a man could be alone, really alone in the dark on one of the big Federal I-jobs. The minute the daylight peeped, there'd be vehicles by the hundreds, by the thousands, scurry-ratting toward the megs, toward this or that foolish occupation. Perhaps it was just the juicing up of his courage for the about-to-be run, but he felt a complete and lofty contempt for the poor landlocked people who used their wheels to go some-where; to go, then stop. Billy had been born in a moving vehicle, had never traveled at a speed below 40 mph to his knowledge, and had never once been off the U.S. of A. Interstate Highway system. You had to say this much for the rotten Ramps: neither had they.

Colonel Tal said, "Billy? On your right hand—"

At the same instant, Jobe Spoiler said, "How do you call it, Billy?"

No time to call it; the pophead merging in from the right in a flare of headlamps was merging all the way, peeling in one, two, three lanes. The little electric runabout, white, and being pushed to the full, had smoke coming off its tires as it bulled over to occupy the same highway space Billy himself was occupying. The runabout was hurtling over like a juggernaut.

19

Billy couldn't veer left or he'd bounce Lee Ramp, and that wouldn't be right, considering the contest challenge already flung. He was in a bind, so he pedaled the brakes and hoped the increased glow of his tails would warn Colonel Tal and Jobe in time.

The popheaded stopper slotted into Billy's space when Billy's brakes grabbed, and the Twister dropped back. Jobe hit him. Brakes screamed. But it was a light smack. Jobe backed off. Billy held onto the wheel, fighting the antique power steering as it recovered from the shock to the frame. It was a minute of terror: Billy checking the rearvision mirror, heartsick as he watched Jobe whipsaw through two lanes, trying to take hold again and avoid slamming Ramp turbines; Billy checking ahead, touching, just caressing the brake with the tip of his half-boot because the runabout driver—crazy girl or woman—her yellow hair burned in the glare, flying and snapping out the left window—kept applying speed, then slacking off, to tease her pursuit. She carried regular state Tin—Nevadas—rather than the Road plates which the government in Washington granted those who lived always moving on the highways.

"You want to get rid of that or shall I?" Lee Ramp said over the radiophone.

"I will," Billy said, shifting up and laying on gas.

He zoomed up behind the runabout, hands tight on the wheel, and gave it a tap from behind, then braked off just enough. The runabout shot ahead as if fired from a cannon. Then suddenly it veered to the right. The right rear tire blew with a loud report. Billy also heard the girl driver shriek as she foolishly went for the brakes.

The runabout did an out-of-control U and came to a shuddering stop with its bonnet crumpled against the right-hand guardrail. Then Billy's Twister was by, and he saw no more.

But he heard another brake-yell, plus some cursing on the radiophone, then more brake-burning, a crash—

Lee Ramp screamed, "Dacey? You all right?"

"This is Werty, Lee. He was runnin' too far to the right. He hit her."

"Drop back, you stupid son of a bitch. Check him."

Headlights in the mirror receded swiftly as the Ramp turbine slowed. Another mammoth over-the-road sign spanning all eight lanes announced the first levels of the Superstack in five miles. The Ramp headlights zoomed up to size again:

"Dacey climbed out. He's walkin'."

"Attaboy, Dacey," Lee breathed, "attaboy, never stop moving, boy. Wasn't your fault—"

And for a moment, Billy could understand. Sympathize. For even if Dacey Ramp were dead, dead in his brains, something in his body would keep him twitching ahead on his feet, then on all fours if need be, because he'd already suffered the supreme humiliation of having his machine slowed to below 40 mph, then stopped; one thing you never did if you were born of the clans was to permit your forward motion to stop.

"You sure bunged that up, Billy," Lee Ramp said, trying to pretend that Dacey's lack of skill hadn't been at fault. Billy stifled a swear word. No point arguing that it was not his skill at fault, but the girl driver's lack of it. And Dacey's; it was worse for a man, the humiliation of coming to a complete halt. No point worrying, either. He had enough on his mind with the nearness of the Superstack—immense, multileveled, built in the vee of slate mountain walls that extended out to the sixteen lanes where Billy was now; the drivers drove down at the bottom between those walls, raising booming echoes.

What about the girl, though?

A stopper, plainly. Joyriding. He hoped he hadn't killed or maimed her. Christ, he hoped he hadn't.

"Billy boy, you cost me one of my good cousins," said Lee Ramp.

"They's only four lanes in the Superstack," said Colonel Tal; he sounded rough; unhappy; and—Billy's palms sweated all at once—none too sure? "What difference does it make?"

"Plenty of difference if you plan to yellow out," Lee returned.

"Did I say we were going to yellow out? Billy exclaimed.

"No, but you didn't say we were running, either."

"There wasn't any time. That silly popheaded—"

"Will you quit making chicken excuses and say yes or no?" Lee yelled.

The radiophone link actually crackled with the noises of the challenge. Billy flinched, then felt ashamed of the unbidden reaction. Why did these Ramps buffalo him? No reason they should; they were all talk and swagger, lacking real skill; why, Colonel Tal could ram them up the wall.

Couldn't he?

Eight lanes, sharply inclined upward, fled beneath the Twister's glimmering orange hood. Like a carrion-eater, old Lee's low, mean turbine stayed on Billy's left, its metal suddenly rippling and flaring as the drivers swept under the first of the blue lamps that brightened the approaches to the Superstack. Windshields shot off stars of light; it was possible to glimpse Lee's profile hunched above his wheel.

About two miles up the slope they reached the chute, the place where the eight lanes began to funnel down to four. The Superstack seemed to climb to the sky, concrete-white, untended in the fastness of the mountains. Billy tried to remember its layout; a double super corkscrew; you went up and around and around, and if you didn't turn off at any of the radials on the way up—other freeways, leading to other places in the western U.S.—then you hit another corkscrew down, rolling tire-hot off the mountains onto the grade leading down to golden California.

But it was all sort of vague now, lacking crisp detail. Possible injury to the stopper in the runabout had densed his thoughts, slowed his perceptions. The rock walls ran away smeary behind him on both sides of his Twister, which had now developed a strange alarming shimmy in the rear end.

He checked the speedo. Godamighty! 94 mph and he didn't even know it.

"Colonel Tal?" he said to the radiophone. "We're going in."

Colonel Tal cleared his throat, archly. "Why, 'course."

"Jobe? We're going in."

Jobe was small-voiced. "Sure." Billy feared for him.

"Okay," Lee Ramp said with another of those wasp-edged chuckles. He spoke to his own clan, "You lads hear that?" They heard. "Okay, now, you drive so Big Daddy would be proud of every one of you."

"Listen, when are you going to stop telling that chicken-shit story that you boys are related to the Hardchargers?" Colonel Tal wanted to know.

"You farty old windbag," Lee answered back, "if Big Daddy was here, he'd *prove* it."

"Don't even believe there *is* a Big Daddy." That was Jobe, making himself sound brave so he would be. Billy squirmed to a tense position in his bucket, held the wheel as tightly as he could. "Don't believe there's even a Hard-charger clan—"

"Is," advised Colonel Tal. "Small and piss-mean, but there is. I've met a few."

"Big Daddy wouldn't wipe his grease rags on you," Lee came back. "He's got fatter nuts to tighten. He's gonna see the Big Fifty before he dies and he can't be bothered with people like you Spoilers. He leaves it to his cousins. He leaves wiping up your kind to us."

Across the connection between the speeding machines, Lee Ramp's laugh sounded like icicles that Billy'd heard snapping on a Vermont power line over the turnpike up there. His eyes crawled to the speedo: an ordinary five places; built to accept 99,999 miles before turning completely. Big Daddy Hardcharger was rumored to have eight places on his custom-modified model. Big Daddy was a maniac—*if* he existed. Death–doomed, the road clans said.

Death. Billy knuckled sweat from his eyes; the wind roaring in the window didn't evaporate it fast enough. He wondered whether he'd see the Firebird this morning.

Colonel Tal refused to lose the last point in the badger-ing game: "If you Ramps—"

Lee cut in, "What say we all kill the mikes and let's get down to some serious driving?" A connection clicked; other clicks followed. The Ramps had shut off. Billy did the same.

The internal combustion machines thundered up the

23

concrete grade. Colonel Tal pulled out to the left of Lee Ramp. Jobe pulled up on Billy's right. The remaining two Ramps flanked the outside.

Hub to hub, the six machines thundered at the chute. The two outside lanes merged out of existence. The drivers were six abreast, in six lanes.

Firebird, Billy thought. *What's it look like, that big red monster trailing flame off its wings?*

Would there be the most beautiful, incredible, cream-breasted naked girl riding it, the bird's blazing back between her bare thighs but not burning them? Billy had his own private conception of the girl some said sat astride the harbinger bird. She was a sweet, clean girl of corn-colored hair and radiant blue eyes; his ideal woman, her clean but voluptuous beauty a contrast to the vengeful look of the burning bird.

I believe there's a Firebird.

No I don't either, it's just some old superstition carried over from a long time ago when there was a hightest gas used it for signs.

But he glanced to the right anyway, up over Jobe's hood past the pearly blue lights; he saw no phantasmal fire-winged thing flying there. He shuddered a little private shudder. He wasn't signed to die just yet.

The way it worked out was, men who were truly men only saw the Firebird the second before the big wheel revolved the last time. As a consequence, nobody in any of the clans had ever actually looked at the hell-red apparition with his own eyes—

A hard bank to the left coming up ahead.

Billy poured on the gas, edging the Twister's bumper out ahead of his flankers. The incline was moderately steep here. The cars streaked into the beginning of the up corkscrew.

Billy was only partially conscious of discrete details: a signboard warning travelers bound for the huge, sprawling Tahoe meg to KEEP RIGHT; another warning to REDUCE SPEED TO 50 MPH. Billy edged the needle up past 95 mph. The Twister began to rattle and yaw in earnest.

Suddenly, on his right, Jobe disappeared.

Quick glance at the rearvision mirror; Jobe was dropping back, his brakelights lighting up the whole tail end of his mother, spilling scarlet along the waxed rear rockerpanels. The highway climbed upward and around to the left, past the radial that shot off through the tunnel to Tahoe. Sound bounced from the high concrete retaining walls. The Ramp car on his right veered over. Instinctively Billy corrected, edged left. He heard his hubs ping Lee Ramp's, corrected again, the steering touchy, slow.

Jobe was out of sight somewhere down in the beginning of the corkscrew behind them. Billy hoped he was all right. He despised Jobe's fear, but he tempered his fury. The kid was only twenty. Billy had two years on him.

Then there wasn't any more time to fret over why Jobe's nerve had gone smash; they were up past the third-level radials; large signs on either side of the lanes zoomed up—

LEFT LANE ENDS   RIGHT LANE ENDS

Fell behind.

Up higher; around, around and up; leftward; force pushed him back against the bucket as he concentrated on steering within the lane markers while his left boot worked the power brake, his right the gas, both helping control his drift in the endless climbing turn. Right and left outside lanes began to narrow, ready to disappear.

Colonel Tal cut it over to the right to scare Lee Ramp. Lee drove steady on, and Colonel Tal looked like he was scared off, whipping back over to his own lane. But he didn't stay there. His purple-flakepainted mother whammed the side of the Ramp on his left; whammed good and hard.

The impact caught the Ramp driver right as his lane ended. He started to put his own squeeze on Tal, trying to edge into Tal's space. But Tal's hit had put him out of control. He went left instead of right, his left front headlamps scraping the concrete retaining wall that angled in where the lanes narrowed.

Sparks and smoke flew. Billy heard tortured metal yammering. The Ramp turbine would bury its nose in the retaining wall unless its driver eased off. He did, with a sudden pound of brakes that dropped him from sight.

So now they were four, roaring in four lanes up past the sixth level where you could glimpse cold stars—if you dared take your eyes off the unreeling twist of concrete. Colonel Tal was on the extreme left; then Lee; then Billy; then the last Ramp. Two and two; an even split.

They held that formation all the way past the Sacramento radial, the LA-Vegas radial, all the rest, to the top.

The four machines burst out along the straightaway at the summit. About one mile of open, guardrailed lanes connected the two corkscrews. The wind whined cold and sharp through the window.

Lee Ramp edged over. Billy wouldn't give. Lee edged back. Billy's speedo read exactly 101 mph. The old mill in the Twister wouldn't take that much punishment for long.

Off on Billy's left, the sky was a steamy orange above the clouds that covered the polluted mountain megs. Dawn; dawn on the great plains. How beautiful.

And how bracing the air. Sweet in the lungs, with just a tang of oil. How fine this feeling, too; this racing toward the down corkscrew with the radials shooting off at all levels, over and under the four main downspiraling lanes —how good, how pure and right it was to be here. There wasn't a sign of a big blazing death-bird keeping pace in the blueblack sky above.

A horn—two horns. Lee's; Colonel Tal's. Billy instinctively turned his head a fraction, saw Colonel Tal inside his mother there beyond Lee's profile. Colonel Tal's old blue-lit face was convulsed with rage.

Billy whipped his head front, suddenly saw the cause of all the horn-blatting. They were roaring into the right-spiraling down incline now. Ahead, showing its tail lamps, was a big, cumbersome wagon bearing Oregon plates. Faces of scared children were pressed to the rear glass. The frantic driver of the wagon couldn't or wouldn't speed fast enough to escape those four thundering machines coming down on his tail, filling all four lanes. The wagon's blinkerlights began to go on and off, *right turn, right turn—*

The wagon slewed into the extreme right lane, trying for the Phoenix radial that led off on the next level below.

26

The wagon almost made it, too; almost. The Ramp turbine on Billy's right clipped its tail end.

Out of control, the wagon skidded down the exit ramp. Instead of following the ramp's curve, the wagon slammed dead ahead into the wall and burst into a fireball whose intensity Billy felt on his bare skin long after they were corkscrewing on down past.

God damn Ramps, he thought, braking, accelerating, working down through the gears when he could afford his brake foot free an instant. *Should of eased off and let that stopper live; poor damn stopper who probably figured he'd beat the monumental dayside traffic by traveling at night.* Out the corner of his right eye, Billy glimpsed the young Ramp whose turbine had done the damage. His mind seethed with foul words. No matter how much honor was up for grabs, Spoilers didn't countenance that kind of blood. But the Ramp—a beaky nose, not much chin— actually looked happy.

They zoomed down past the fifth level. Billy banged over and handed the Ramp kid a good stiff rap. Give him credit—the youngster held on tight. Billy wobbled back into his own lane, fighting for control. Damn power steering never had been any good. Always needed over-correcting—

Lee Ramp recognized the signs of Billy's distress, and took advantage. He wrenched to the right, pasted Billy's Twister a hard one in the side. As if it were a pre-arranged strategy, the Ramp on Billy's right dropped back suddenly. He steered into Billy's lane, directly behind the Twister, as if he knew something would happen to Billy's machine—

It did; it started to skid to the right. The rear end started flipping around out of control.

Lee Ramp rushed on by and down around out of sight. The retaining wall loomed dead ahead. Billy twisted the wheel left just as his machine started to rise on its left side. She wouldn't come around fast enough.

His right fender hit the wall, scraped, peeled completely off. He heard the yell of metal. Suddenly his correcting worked. The Twister pulled away from the wall; its left tires came down, bam, but didn't blow. Then Billy was weaving on down through the corkscrew.

He still had trouble steering. When he turned the wheel too far, the right front tire whined. Obviously part of the body metal was crimped in dangerously close to the tire.

Cutting it? Slashing it?

His eyes fell on the speedo. 65 mph. Falling. *Never below 40 mph!* Sweet God! A man wasn't a man who let that happen!

He geared, got it wrong, threw it in properly an instant after the tire-whine, and continued on down the corkscrew. The others—two Ramps, Colonel Tal—were long gone ahead.

All at once Billy grew conscious of a gumminess in his right eyesocket. He swiped his eye with his right hand, examined his fingers. In the blue roadway lights they shone stickyblack.

How'd he been banged that way? When had it happened? In the frozen seconds in which he'd skated away from the wall? He hadn't even felt an impact.

Driving cautiously, he made it down past the first level and into the plum shadows of the western grade leading to California.

About a mile ahead he saw Colonel Tal's red tails. The Colonel's mother was going list-and-bump, list-and-bump, the left rear tire in ribbons. But the old hard charger was driving a good minimum 45 mph nonetheless.

Farther on down the grade, two other sets of tails receded quite fast. Billy's throat filled with bile.

He caught up with Colonel Tal, dodging in and out among a convoy of bullet-shaped milk freighters to do it. He pulled up alongside the Colonel's mother. The Interstate was seven lanes each way now. He flipped on the radiophone.

"Lose a tire, Colonel?"

"Yes, sir, I did, and that's when they lost me. You all right?"

"Got a fenderwell about to rip through a tire, but if I keep her bearing ever so little left I think I can make it."

Colonel Tal made a phlegmy sound. "Lee let me have the middle finger nice and proper before they barreled away."

"That bastard." Hot-faced, Billy searched the shadows far down the grade. But the Ramp lights had disappeared.

"I think they killed that poor stopper in the Superstack," he said.

"They're really a chickenshit bunch," Colonel Tal agreed. "Ought to be stopped in place one of these days, every last one."

"Lee will be. Nobody beats me more than once."

The phlegmy sound again. "Hope you remember that."

Billy chewed his lip. "How'd they take us?"

"I reckon it was bad driving on our part and orneriness on theirs."

"Spoilers don't suffer that kind of hurrah, Colonel Tal."

"Stop saying it, Billy. Just remember it silent. Inside."

Rebuked, Billy shut up.

Turbine and electric cars from the meg fringe towns at the foot of the grade began to fill the superhighway. They came in at cautious speed from the right-hand feeders. Already the groves to either side of the great elevated road were tinged with light off the mountains. Well, Billy wouldn't forget. Billy'd remember, yes indeed he would. He'd meet up with Lee Ramp again, too. It was inevitable. There weren't that many clans on the highways.

The clans represented about ten percent of the total U.S. population, so the government said. They met on regular occasions—at holidays like Christmas—and when Billy saw Lee Ramp again, he vowed he'd smile and hide the knife till the right moment.

"'Spose we better head back and hunt for Jobe," Colonel Tal suggested. "He was moving, but not very fas—holy waters of Jordan!"

So excited was Tal that Billy automatically looked left. He saw the Colonel staring at him in the new-breaking daylight across the space that separated their mothers. Billy was acutely conscious of being on policed roadway in a wholly illegal, unsafe, air-polluting internal combustion machine, and that fear gnawed him when he spotted Colonel Tal's gap-jawed expression.

"What's wrong, Colonel?"

Over the radiophone the answer: "Your face. It's black as oil."

"Cut myself somehow."

"Then let's not stand on ceremony, boy. It's pick up Jobe and back to the clan."

At the next loop-back, they crossed and spurted eastward up the grade, passing Jobe who was still heading west. Jobe looped back and caught up with them as they slacked off going down from the Superstack on the eastern side of the mountain. Shortly they drew up on six vans of Rollbars riding the magnetic strip. An immense egg-shaped fuel truck rode the lane just to the left of one of the Rollbar haulers. The egg-shaped truck bore the gaudy logotype of a national oil company. Hoses ran between supplier and receiver in three places.

Billy drove steadily ahead, passing one of the communal vans. Some Rollbar kids were already up and frolicking on one of the little porches with which each living space was equipped. The kids hollered and waved. Billy was so preoccupied, he didn't feel like waving back. He was still thinking of Lee Ramp. Of settling.

Limping, off the top pace but still traveling an acceptable speed, the three mothers weaved in and out of morning traffic thickening at the sun-drenched base of the divide. An hour later, the rearmost of the twenty-eight Spoiler residence and service vans came into sight.

Billy sprinted ahead, going by men in sports shirts driving little two-passenger jobs, and men in Wrinkleproof suits off to some cubicle in one of the cities buried under those sorry gray clouds in the east. As Billy passed, steering deftly—his ripped-open forehead had finally started to hurt but the pain braced him—most of the men gave him a strange, shuddery fisheye. For there were not all that many road clans visible in the country; not all that many of these weird nomads whose home was no territorial state as such, but all the ten- and twelve- and fourteen- and sixteen-lane highways of America, by decree of the Federal government. Yes, Wrinkleproof in the blue electric Billy was passing actually gawked at the special Road license plate on Billy's mother. By rights, he should have kept plates off an illegal car. But what

30

were you without your Tin, your badge, to identify you to those lucky—or unlucky—enough to see you howling through the night on a run?

Nobody in that wagon full of stoppers had lived to remember the Road plates on the Ramp turbine, Billy bet. God damn. The sting of needing to settle became doubly deep, doubly strong.

All of a sudden he felt a wetness in his crotch. Blood. So much blood he was black with it.

No wonder he'd been cruising in a weird, euphoric state, wondering occasionally with a far part of his mind why he seemed to see the sunlit highway through black rain. Drops of blood clung to his eyebrows. The whole front of his head hurt.

Evidently Colonel Tal had recognized the seriousness of the injury where Billy, because of shock, had not. Dimly he heard the older man's voice interconnected with the clan vans ahead "—climb on the Fed band, Eudora. Find the nearest wheeldoc."

"I'm reading you, Colonel. Will do it pronto." The woman's voice was coarse, basso: "You limping in?"

"That's right, we had a little howl with a couple of Ramps."

"Ramps? Thought they were bound for Illinois for Christmas."

" 'Pears we all heard they were someplace else. You can't shake a hex, I guess."

"You want me to call the service man out of line?"

"Naw," Tal drawled, "we just want to pussy along in these mothers till it's bright as noon and we get spotted by the Federals."

"Sorry, Colonel. Will do it pronto."

"That's all right, Eudora, you just ought to know better."

Colonel Tal took the point, Jobe the rear. That allowed Billy the safest spot, in the middle. They traveled up the highway at about 45 mph, holding in the second lane from the right. The extreme right lane was occupied by the caravan of clan vehicles, twenty-eight big, multitired, multitiered vans which now, one by one, unhooked from the magnetized strips buried in the roadbed.

First the rearmost van unhooked, its speed slacking

31

off from the standard Federally approved 80 mph. The van slowed down till its speed matched those of the three mothers. Then the van second from the rear unhooked. In minutes, the whole caravan was once more rolling at the same speed, only slower than it had been before.

A van fifth from the rear blinkered its way over into the lane in which Colonel Tal and the others were driving. Across the back doors of the van, large, cheerfully-colored letters said:

SAMMY SPOILER
MOBILE SERVICE AND PARTS
EXPERT MAINTENANCE OF ALL MODELS

The rear doors opened. Inside, the van was two-level; the effect was much like looking into the side of a house whose wall had been peeled away. The upper level was the garage proper. There, several men in coveralls were waving. The lower level appeared gloomy, like a grease pit. This was storage space for nearly a dozen illegal mothers belonging to various Spoiler boys. From the rear end of the van, powered ramps descended at an angle, hit the concrete to drag and shoot off sparks.

Colonel Tal zoomed his mother ahead, wobbling badly on the mangled rim. But he was a top man at the wheel; he maneuvered his front end till it was lined up with the ramps dragging from the van's rear. Then he accelerated.

His front tires hit the ramps. The hood tilted upward. The grabbers had him. His mother was pulled up the ramp and into the dark lower level.

Billy's turn next. He wiped his eyes, only managing to blind himself with blood. He saw a long, sharp strut sticking out through the cracked vinyl of one of the antique windshield visors. The strut must've gouged a trench in his head at some point. He felt wobbly in the belly and genitals. He pressed the gas pedal. The Twister edged forward toward the van.

He recognized friendly, familiar faces on the upper level. The men in coveralls kept waving, encouraging him.

But his hands were slippery on the wheel. The front end whipsawed as he pulled up on the dragging ramps. He backed off just in time.

He swallowed, gnawed his lower lip a while, then tried again. His front wheels bounced up on the ramps. One wheel started to skid toward the raised edge. Billy twisted the steering wheel right—

The grabbers on the ramps caught, pulled. His mother angled upward. He enjoyed the rest of the ride, the short ride up into the channels in the smelly belly of the service van. He nosed the Twister extra gently against the rear of Colonel Tal's machine. The older man was just climbing out.

Billy heard Jobe's mother come in behind. The van doors clanged. There were footsteps all over the catwalks above; Spoilers rushing to find out what had transpired.

"Won't forget," Billy said to nobody special. Colonel Tal rapped on his windshield. Billy paid no attention. "Won't forget."

Colonel Tal bent to say something. He was being pressed from the back by jawing Spoilers—women, little kids, Uncle Sammy and his service crew. Tal tapped the glass again. "Hey, boy!"

Billy was too tired and blinded by blood. He relaxed in the bucket and fainted.

Sometime during that morning, Eudora Spoiler, who acted as the caravan communications chief, got on the radiophone wavebands and located a mobile doc. The nearest was cruising about three hours away, in the desert near the huge Vegas meg. Without so much as taking a vote—one of their number had been injured, after all—the twenty-eight vehicles peeled off onto a north-south ten-lane, then hooked to the magnetized strips and switched on the immense air-conditioning units built into each of the vans as part of their year-round climate control equipment.

By the time Vegas began to shimmer on the 110-degree horizon, the caravan consisted of the twenty-eight vans plus a couple dozen two- and four-seaters which normally nested in the family vans. The smaller machines, com-

33

pletely legal and equipped with the full complement of safety and pollution control devices, were driven by married men, usually with their wives beside them and kids, if any, romping in the back. All the personal cars bore one similar identification mark; they were all products of General Ford Motors.

The wheeldoc drove an elongated electric painted white with blue crosses. He pulled up alongside the general service van. Speaking with Eudora via radiophone, he synched his speed. Extensor arms from the side of the general service van locked padded clamps onto special docking fixtures on the right side of his electric. The doc punched his machine into neutral. Freewheeling, it was borne alongside the much larger vehicle.

The extensors retracted, pulling the electric flush to the specially scooped side of the van. Seals on the doc's electric locked rubbery-tight against seals on the port that opened in the van's outer wall. The doc's right door rolled back and recessed inside the rear window. Crouching over, the doc was able to move from his machine to the van without so much as a leak of a single whiff of supercooled air from either vehicle.

The doc treated Billy's deeply gashed forehead, restored his spirits a little—a little—with a happy blue pill, rendered his punchcard, and departed with a wave. The doc's electric unlocked, then sped off toward the horizon-spanning glow of Vegas twinkling in the desert dusk. Billy watched through a port in the wall.

He was lying in a bunk in the van's hospital section. He was alone in the ward; all the other bunks were empty. As the Nevada twilight came on, he wondered why he felt so bad that he wanted to cry; he wondered whether he'd ever feel good again.

The malaise continued till the happy blue pill took effect. He dropped off to the comforting rumble of the van moving, always moving along the concrete. At least a man could rely on some things never changing.

The following day, no worse off except for a head bandage, he resumed his regular four-hour-a-day job in Sammy Spoiler's repair van. That evening, at his own expense, he radiophoned Western Traffic Central—a five-mile-wide bunker somewhere under the Rockies—and after lengthy delays, found out that the girl in the white runabout had not been seriously injured. She'd been jailed for being popheaded on heavy drugs, though.

The fact that she was alive didn't dispel his gloom. Nor did working on his Twister on his own time: battering out the rippled metal; welding on a new fender torched from one that didn't fit; hand-rubbing each primer coat, then applying a finish coat of matching orange. All the while, the hours, the days, streamed together in a lightheaded, unreal way. He was alternately hot and cold. Felt strange pains in his groin, sudden upsurges of his pulse. Avoided the cafeteria van at the usual hours for meals. Colonel Tal Spoiler brought up the subject one night during the first week in December.

The caravan, which had grown to near fifty Spoiler vans and twice as many satellite runabouts, sedans, wagons, was loafing through the moss-hung Louisiana delta, generally aiming east. Billy had avoided dinner again tonight. Instead, he'd gone over to the general store van when it docked for half an hour alongside the bachelors' van. He purchased a pint of Lightnin'. He took it to the little two-by-four porch with which each outside cubicle was equipped.

Partitions separated Billy's porch from those on the levels below and above, and those on his right and left along the same level. There was barely room for him to scrooch his aluminum chair into a corner and prop his bare feet up on the rail. He watched the live oaks go by, dusky in the heat and buzz of early evening.

A knock.

He glanced up, a pale, slender boy with a wash of ordinary brown hair hanging down to his eyes. He had his mother's gray eyes—she had been a Tollbooth—and a large nose inherited from his father, who had died at age 43 in an accident on the Detroit Triple Beltway.

They pulled his father from the wreckage just moments after death. His right leg was still jamming up and down as if to operate the accelerator pedal. Even near death

35

old Frank Townes Spoiler, originally of Chattanooga, had tried to keep driving.

There were three Spoilers in the rescue party, Billy heard tell. He'd been off with the main body of the clan when it happened; he was still young enough to be at studies then. Minimum education was eight grades in the school van; the government didn't insist on more for the clans. It had problems enough without insisting.

Anyway, of the three men who pulled Frank T. Spoiler's body out of the smashed machine, two experienced severe mental disorders, and one died of heart failure in an hour as a result of having been forced to stop—stop to a standstill, not just below 40 mph—in order to pull Frank T. Spoiler out. Billy was always glad that his father's leg had been jerking even after he expired. He bragged about this occasionally when he was drunk. His mother had a stroke two months after the accident, and that was that. An only child, Billy had been on his own ever since.

The knock again. Billy waved the plasto pint of Lightnin'. "Didn't I say come on in?"

"Didn't hear you, boy." Colonel Tal squeezed from the gloom of the living cubicle—Billy left the lights off a lot lately—and wedged into the other corner of the porch. "Naw, don't get up. I don't need a chair, I won't be that long."

The Colonel had a cracked old face, bushy brows, and a certain secret keenness in his eyes which those in the clan attributed to his twelve grades of education. The Colonel removed his broad-brimmed white hat and fanned the air moving past his chin.

"Mighty muggy down here. Should grow a mite more dry and pleasant once we hit Florida."

Billy extended the Lightnin' pint. "Have some?"

"No, thanks. Had liver trouble lately. Tryin' to lay off."

Colonel Tal had never called on Billy privately before. The situation made him nervous. He struggled for things to say. "Is there going to be the usual gathering for Christmas?"

Colonel Tal spat over the porch rail. Down on the next level, a bachelor Spoiler let out a good-natured yell. A

36

girl giggled. Billy felt a painful twitch in his crotch. The great van tires hummed on.

"Yes, this Christmas promises to be the largest ever," the older man said. "Rally point's the Florida state line. There'll be three glorious weeks of cruisin' and relaxin' with all bad feelings forgot." Tal picked his teeth, examined his fingernail. "As you know, I personally never drive solo during one of these wingdings. Nor sober up till Twelfth Night, either. Ought to do your spirits good too, Billy."

The Lightnin' rasped down Billy's throat. "You think my spirits need perking, Colonel Tal?"

"I'm not one to intrude, Billy boy, you certainly know that. But I was havin' a bite with Uncle Sammy in the cafeteria van this noon, and he said your work hasn't even been par lately."

Billy slammed his feet down on the little porch. "He can tell me."

"Oh, horsepoop, boy, don't get up on your hinds. He's not sore. He's worried about you. In fact lots o' folks have been noticing how you've funked around since the morning we ran with the Ramps. I'm not as tactful as most. Being ornery as hell and twice as old, I have certain patriarchal rights." Billy didn't know what *patriarchal* meant, but when Colonel Tal pronounced it, it sounded impressive. "One of them is coming in here and giving you some advice and counsel, being as how you've no mother, father, brother or sister to call your own."

"I don't feel lonesome," Billy countered. "All the Spoilers are my kin, right?"

Colonel Tal regarded the ghostly live oaks passing at the superhighway's edge. "Take comfort in that technicality if you wish. At times it can be a comfort indeed. But we're both smart enough to know that nobody in the Spoiler clan—let alone any of the other clans—is honest to God clearly and unequivocally related. Past the first generation, anyway. Your mom and dad, they were married, sure. Beyond that—" A genteel shrug; another pick of the teeth. "It's anybody's guess."

Billy wondered at the point the older man was reaching. But he suppressed his grumpiness that sprang from some

37

hollow, lonesome core of him. He let Colonel Tal prod him a little more. "You know we're all related but nobody knows how, right?"

Billy felt cloudy from the Lightnin'. He waved the pint. "Teacher said something once in school, I recollect. But what, exactly—" He shrugged.

"We're a mighty proud and fiercely loyal bunch, Billy my boy. Started out that way years ago—oh, long before that chickenshit Chinee war began. Maybe fifty years ago? The old auto and motorbike clubs an' clans stuck together. Nobody was blood kin to anybody else. But once the clans started livin' on the road and travelin' in groups, like with like, things changed. Not having much education—" A sniff, was it? "—to keep proper records, when a couple got hitched, their children remembered but their grandchildren didn't. And when some little bastard needed a name, it was took from the great American roadside we know and love almost better'n we love that old time religion."

A grandiloquent gesture. The wind changed and Billy smelled gin. Despite protests about liver trouble, Colonel Tal was potted.

"—true and authentic family names, Billy. Names from the great land, the Peels and the Rallyes and the Rollbars and the Afterburners and so on and so forth—"

Colonel Tal coughed. He wiped an excess of spit from his lips, with no visible embarrassment.

"All of which, my laddybuck, says that we are none of us your *exact* kin, but we are all of us your *general* kin, and therefore we fret about your state, get me?"

"I'll be fine," Billy eventually replied.

"I'd say you had spring frog fever but it ain't spring."

Suddenly Billy popped his head up. "You know damn well—"

"No, I don't. What is it, boy?" Colonel Tal's eyes burned. "Being bested by Lee Ramp?"

"What else?"

"There'll come a time—you vowed—"

"A time—sure. But when? It can't come soon enough for me!"

With one gulp, Billy wiped out the rest of the Lightnin'.

38

He flung the plasto pint out past the side of the van. It hit water in a ditch beside the freeway, and a pink and white feathered waterbird rose, flapping ungracefully. Billy fantasized a Firebird.

Following a belch, Colonel Tal cleared his throat. "Well, I can appreciate your feelings. However, I think you dwell on it too much. Everything in its own good time—the sowing and the reaping, the planting and the harvesting. We'll fix the son of a bitch. Meanwhile, I've concluded you shouldn't be so alone. No mom and pop, no other for-certain kin—that tends to make a man broody."

Colonel Tal reached over and laid a hand on Billy's shoulder. There was no drunkenness in that hand, only hard flesh, strong veins, old scars white against deep brown. The hands of a hard charger.

"How old are you, boy? Exactly?"

"Twenty-three now."

"Isn't good for a man your age to be alone. It's time you hunted up a woman."

"Listen, Colonel, I've had my share of gash, so don't—"

"Not that kind of woman, lamebrain. A sweet, permanent woman."

"Who you just happen to have in your pocket?"

"No, I don't. But there'll be plenty hanging around when all the clans lock vans for the Florida cruise. So I want to ask you a favor."

"What is it?"

"When the holiday comes, shine up your smile and slick your hair and try hard to take an interest." Colonel Tal's voice faded away, then resumed against the counterpoint of the great tires. "Your glooms are casting a bad air over the caravan, Billy. I was asked to speak to you about it, and I've done it. I've given you my best solution. Pull yourself out of the pits. Be your old self, won't you? I mean—" The wise eyes bored in. "I came here for a promise, boy."

Billy felt resentful. That faded. Somehow, it was a balm to say, "Okay, Colonel. I promise."

Colonel Tal thanked him and went away as the van running lights came on. Later that night, Billy had an aggravating and frightening wet dream involving himself, the Firebird, and the honey-haired blonde who rode the bird with flames streaming out behind her naked buttocks. He awoke and thrashed and swore. After a while, he relaxed. He'd promised Colonel Tal. The promise relieved him of worry about choices. He did want to fulfill the promise, too. The clan really did mean a lot to him. Almost as much as his Twister.

He zipped back the port at the head of his bunk. Beyond his porch, sunlight glittered on bayou water. The sunlight looked warm and pleasant. He smiled for the first time in a long while.

A slap of the counter. "Mr. Jonas Spoiler, sir?"

"Yes, sir, I—well, goddam!" laughed the little man as he turned from his sales shelves. "Billy! You haven't been on these premises in quite a spell." He gave Billy's trousers a mock glance of reproof. "Your threadbares show it, too."

"I'm here to do something about that, Mr. Jonas Spoiler."

The little fellow winked. "Two hundred miles from the Florida border—I guess it's time! Figure to cut a step with some of that gash from the other clans?"

"Figure to cut more than a step."

"Ol' swordsman Billy. Like father, I always say. Your poppa, now, he was the one. Oh, he had them. How he did." Jones bustled around and gripped Billy's arm and guided him to the far side of the haberdashery van, which was actually divided into two levels: lower for men's, upper for women's and children's. "Now I think what you need to appear real smart is what the highway delivery service just stocked me with two days ago." Pudgy hands reached for a garment on a rack. "My special Dacro-prest Imitation Kentucky Denim two-piece Sunday suit. How do you like this here slate blue shade?"

"Mighty handsome," said Billy, for it was; he admired the raked lapels, the triple venting. They were wearing those in Nashville, if he recalled the telly right. "Let me try it on."

Jonas's grin matched his customer's. "Yes, *sir.*" The van rolled on through the morning toward Florida.

From the border and the first state-planted palms, two hundred and forty vans rolled south at a leisurely 60 mph. They rolled three and four abreast on the six-lane super.

Cars with up-north tags whizzed around them, bound for the tropical south and a quickie vacation. The northern drivers gawked at the sight of so many road clan vans not only together, a palette of rainbow paints, but actually locked three and four side by side, with free access between. Whether vans traveled singly or in multiples, doors between were never locked. In fact outer doors of the larger vans were never locked at all. Anyone could come in or go out any time.

At such a festive season, the law was inclined to be forgiving about so many vans blocking so many lanes. Also, the law knew there'd be little or no wild driving. Generally the vans remained hooked into the magnetic strips, and the communications chief of each clan took care to advise the nearest post of the Federal Highway Patrol that a party was in progress, and would be until after New Year's.

More Spoilers came in from Tennessee. There was a complement of Holidays—offshoots of those who fancied the name Holiday Inn—and there were a few Johnsons in orange-roofed vans, and a couple of vans of Clover-leafs and even a Ramp or two.

Two nights after the border rendezvous, they were all down below Orlando. Four of the vans were opened into one large mobile hall; they were special vans with knockdown partitions, used as schoolrooms most of the time. The women of the clans, and their young ones, put on a hastily rehearsed Christmas pageant.

How sweet *O Little Town of Bethlehem* sounded on the portable electronic pipeorgan, electronic guitar and traps. A spotlight shone on the infant Jesus in His crib. A Johnson lady seated near Billy fanned herself with a palm leaf and remarked that the infant was a Johnson, not three days old. The Magi wore Dacro-prest sleeping robes, and at the finish, the entire audience sang *Silent*

41

Night, and many wept. Billy, all slicked hair and honed creases—he was wearing his new Imitation Denim Sunday suit—felt touched with saving grace, plus a vague yearning for a return to innocence.

After the pageant, the meditation was delivered by a divine named Reverend Cleatus Cloverleaf. He inveighed against the moral rot that had set in among those who did not dwell forever mobile on the roadways of America; he called down damnation on the heads of those who still fought for birth control legislation; he branded as heretical liars those who wailed that the U.S. population was reaching crush point:

"They say we—brothers and sisters of the road—are the very proof, shunted off to live upon wheels and the government dole, so we will not crowd the already over-crowded land. But I say that is a blasphemous lie! We chose the road openly. That is, our forebears did. They chose the music of the wheels and of the motors. They came on to the highways of their own free will, and not as the result of some social-tinkering plan! And that is exactly the way we still feel today!"

Applause, cheers.

The approval inspired Reverend Cloverleaf to take off on the softbellies who, for decades, had been advocating an end to the Pan-asian War. He called them unpatriotic lunatics, or worse; the same kind as would deliver the big lie about their being no more habitable urban space in America:

"Have we not found space and freedom beneath the singing wheels of our machines? Is there not room for all upon the turnpikes and freeways? Room for those red-blooded, God-fearing men and women whose forebears, amongst the beloved hills and piney woods, first heard the thunder of superchargers on the roadways of the night? We have dwelled on the road in many cases as long as twenty years plus twenty without committing the sin of stopping—the sin of traveling below 40 mph—the sin of exiting from life's never ending turnpike. There is no sinful coercion upon us. Of our own free choice, we heed God's message and follow the clean, open life on wheels!"

This harangue produced even more enthusiastic audience response. Billy joined in, but he was also busy looking around trying to catch a glimpse of a glinting hair-sprayed head, a roguish smile.

But he saw nothing; no girl who exactly touched him the right way. He began to feel depressed again as Reverend Cloverleaf skewed his message back to the infant Jesus. The service came to an end with a rousing *Hark the Herald*.

Leaving with the crowd, Billy noticed an interesting brunette-crowned face in among a bunch of Johnson boys. Then he got a look at her figure. Whew! He'd break a promise to the infant Jesus, Himself, rather than ask a girl that fat to dance.

Fingering the creases on his Dacro-prest Imitation Denim and smelling the smell of his own STP Brand All-Man Afta-shave Bracer, he let the crowd drift him along aimlessly, without plan. Without hope, it seemed like.

Starting at midnight, the four interlocked vans were turned into a festive dance hall. Tables decked with plastic evergreen appeared at the perimeter. The tables were laden with fried chickens, the trimmings, and great cut glass bowls of ruby colored punch that foamed periodically as new batches were added. A few of the bowls were straight; most were loaded with corn liquor brewed specially for the occasion. The young combo on an improvised dais struck up noisy, amplified mountainpop and the dancing began.

His skull afire after two cups of punch, Billy lingered in a corner watching the dancing couples. Across the hall, Colonel Tal eyed him. Billy glanced away.

Immaculate in yellow Imitation Denim, Jobe Spoiler scuttled up from behind:

"Hey there, Billy."

"Have a drink, Jobe. And tell me when you spot the choicest gash in the whole party, will you?"

His eyes roved. He smelled perfume, watched shimmering hair and young girl thighs. Nothing sparked him.

"You won't want a drink when you hear the news. There's Ramps docked outside. Maybe two, three dozen."

Billy shrugged. "Christmas is truce time. It's the rule."

"Yeh, but Uncle Sammy whispered that one of 'em crashing the party was—"

Jobe stopped. Billy's face had become peculiar indeed. It was slicked with sweat.

Perhaps half way down the hall, beneath a flush of magenta and green holiday lanterns, a girl was talking with a group of boys about Billy's age. Billy stared and stared. His hand was tight and white on his punch glass. Suddenly Billy pushed the glass into Jobe's unbidden hand.

"Hold this."

As he walked the distance to the group, the sweating of his palms grew worse. His heart picked up speed. He could feel it in his chest, lubbing hard. He was seized by a compulsion to turn back. Just then the girl looked straight at him across the shoulder of a boy pawing her arm.

She looked away. Then she looked back. She shaped her mouth into the most dazzling, surprised, lovely smile Billy'd ever seen. Her eyes were green; her mouth was large; it made her smile blinding.

Then all at once she stopped smiling. As though she'd been hurt. Billy's insides wrenched. He thought he felt the floor of the van hall shift. The combo, an electronic fiddle added now, screamed its mountainpop.

He still had eight or ten feet before he reached the loud bunch of boys. All of them seemed to be handling the girl, poking her, teasing her, twisting the sleeve of her ruffled white party dress. Abruptly the girl ducked her head away, changed position so she could no longer meet Billy's eyes. Her smile came back. Her laughter glided up the scale, girlish and teasing.

She patted the cheek of the boy nearest her. The pat looked a little hard, reproving. With a sullen grin and an over-the-shoulder remark, the boy walked off.

Godamighty she's beautiful, Billy thought, walking faster. She was: slender, almost frail, with high, small breasts, and a sky-blue ribbon in taffy hair worn long, to her waist. He didn't care for the way she teased and patted and gripped the hand of one attentive boy, then another. In a chaotic way, he recognized womanly skills with which he, no fast talker, was unprepared to cope.

44

Up came her head again; her green eyes stared there, beneath the magenta holiday lanterns that lent her soft, pale skin a blush. She stared another second that was long as time. Then she glanced away. But he saw the corners of her mouth turn up.

A smile? For me? He was hot-headed, dizzy. He was afraid. But he couldn't turn back. He extended his hand past the nearest boy.

Conversation stopped.

A single clogged word was all he could push out. "Dance?"

Her voice was low, sweet. "Why, thank you. But can't you see there are a lot of others in line?" She said it with pride, telling him where to get off.

Or seeing whether he would?

He didn't like the woman ways he saw in her green eyes. But the heat inside him pushed that aside. He kept his hand stuck out in the air, wiggling his fingers a little. "But this one's a slow one. My kind. Come on."

Near his shoulder, he felt unpleasant eyes. They belonged to a puffy-faced, overdressed boy he thought was a Cloverleaf. The boy said, "If Rose Ann says it isn't her pleasure—"

Billy stiffened noticeably. The eyes of all the boys turned to glittery glass under the green and magenta lanterns. Suddenly Rose Ann bobbed her head. She turned sideways, slipped between two boys, closed her soft fingers around Billy's with a quick pressure. "But it is my pleasure. I just decided."

The woman-teasing was gone from her green eyes. Heat remained.

She smelled of lilac scent. Color glowed in her cheeks as she walked beside him to the edge of the dancing area. He was conscious of her watching him out of the corner of her eye.

"I'm afraid I don't even know your name, though I saw you with some Spoilers a while ago."

"My name's Billy. Billy Spoiler."

"I'm Rose Ann Holiday."

He turned to the music, began to stamp and shuffle into

45

the beat of the languorous broken-hearted mountainpop ballad. Rose Ann turned too, a yard separating them. They began to dance in the fashion of the other couples, hands and feet moving, bodies not touching.

"Never seen you at a Christmas do before," Billy said.

"My papa wouldn't let me come till I was seventeen."

"It's your first one?"

"Yes, and I just love it. Truly." Sure; hadn't he seen all those admirers?

"You—" He could barely speak. "You be here for the whole run?"

"My papa said we would, right through the New Year."

She moved, her hips gliding one way, then another, then back, her beautiful face changing and reflecting the patterns of the festive lanterns. Billy kept time somehow, though not with the fluidity that she had. The music curled around in his brain, the loveliest, sweetest melody he'd ever heard, even though he'd never heard the song before. He drowned in her lilac scent.

"That's good," he managed to say. "You're a pretty one, Miss Rose Ann."

Green eyes said, *Count yourself lucky.* "Why, thanks. I've been told that's true."

You be careful, Billy warned himself. He sensed a mean streak in her somewhere, born of her awareness of her natural grace, her looks, the way her hair whipped gently from side to side as she danced, capable of exciting a man to a frenzy.

The music kept rippling through his blood. All at once he felt himself with the rhythm, with *her,* stepping better, right on the beat. Color came up in her cheeks again. Their eyes locked. They danced.

It went on, and on, hurling him around, soaring him high, dropping him low. Self-contained, he saw little if anything of those outside. He and Rose Ann turned and stepped to the sad, lovely music inside a bubble of magic holiday lights.

She danced with her arms extended at her shoulders. Her fingers snapped but made no sound. Her eyes looked

46

straight to his, her small breasts up tight inside the frill white of her party dress. It went on, it went on—

Then it stopped. It was a moment before he realized.

She reached across quickly, squeezed his hand.

"Thanks a lot, Billy. That was real nice."

He grabbed her elbow. "Rose Ann, I want to see you—"

She eased away, but not angrily. "Well, that might be nice—" Then her green eyes caught something in back of him. Her mouth went to an O for a second. Something was wrong. He turned around.

Among the admiring boys from whom he'd pulled her—they all looked smug now; they were laughing and punching each other—stood a tall, lank-haired young man in a wrinkled old velveteen party coat with black edged lapels, bleached-out 'tans and heavy road boots.

Rose Ann indicated Lee Ramp. "Oh! There's my boyfriend."

Rocks rained on Billy; a landslide in a second. She saw, moved in close to brush his arm with her breast, whisper, "I mean, he *thinks* he is. I guess he is, sometimes. But that doesn't mean I'm his *property*—"

Green eyes, game-playing, saying, *Do you understand?* "Come on."

She took his hand, fingers clenching tight. She walked close by him so that their hands were pressed between their moving thighs. Billy felt a moment of terror; Lee Ramp didn't miss the intimacy.

What kind of girl is this? he thought. *What does she want? I think she's playing around with me. Just like with all the rest*—

Somehow it didn't matter.

They left the dance floor, Rose Ann actually pulling him till he composed himself and caught up, struggling not to show by his stride or his face that he was afraid. What had seemed so beautiful a minute ago now showed all the signs of coming apart into catastrophe.

Then, just out of earshot of Lee Ramp and the boys who had fallen silent, gleefully anticipating a showdown, Rose Ann whispered again, "I want you to see me. My

47

papa's name is Belcher Holiday. You can find the van if you ask anybody—"

One hip thrust out and thumbs in his belt loops, big-man style, Lee Ramp said loudly, "Enjoy your dance, Billy?"

Billy licked his lips. "Very good, thanks."

"My girl's a pretty fine dancer. Pretty fine other ways, too." Rose Ann dropped her head down; Billy hurt. Rose Ann's reaction told him that what Lee Ramp said must be true.

Billy's anger began to build. "Yeh," he said, "I know."

Lee's eyes jumped. "About the dancing, is what you mean."

"Did I say anything else?"

Lee let his gaze rest on Billy a long, contemptuous moment. Then he shrugged.

"Guess you didn't. Better you didn't, either. This is Christmas." He was easy and grinning all of a sudden; in his glance Billy saw the Calneva Superstack. Lee knew he saw it. The wickedness between them crackled.

"Well," said Lee, "now you've had your minute of fun, I think it's my turn to dance with her." He grabbed Rose Ann's hand. She tried to pull away. Lee held fast. She bobbed her head.

"I'm tired, Lee. I want some punch."

"But I want to dance, honey."

"I'm thirsty, Lee."

"After we dance," he said, jerking her hand so that she lurched against his side. He wrapped his arm around her waist and pulled her along toward the floor, where a mean, heavy mountainpop stomp had struck up.

Rose Ann managed one glance back at Billy. He thought it said, *I don't like this. Please don't think I like this—*

Then she was gone, Lee holding her hard as they went into the fierce, foot-pounding dance.

Behind Billy, one of the admirers snickered.

"Lee said he ran you real good through the Superstack, Spoiler."

Hating, Billy didn't turn. He didn't dare. If he did, he'd fight.

Another boy: "Give ol' Lee credit. He isn't any kind of mean winner. Why, while he was watching you, he said that at least you were better with your footwork than under the wheel. That's something for a tough buck like Lee to—"

Billy swung, glared. The speaker swallowed, then halfway grinned.

Billy wanted to hit, pound, attack. He didn't. He walked away, sick with knowing how close to a fracas his hate had carried him.

The great tires hummed. He felt sweaty, itchy, rolling from side to side in his bunk.

He didn't like Rose Ann Holiday. There was a streak in her that bothered him all the way to the bottom of his mind.

But he couldn't stop thinking of her because he was in love with her.

He didn't sleep all night.

"Rose Ann?"

"Mmm?"

"You sure Lee's still down driving the Keys?"

"You keep asking that like you're afraid of him or something, Billy."

"No, I'm not," he half lied. "I just don't want this to be busted up. It's too damn nice."

"Well, you ought to stop your worrying, don't you think?"

"Guess so."

"Know so. I've met you every night since the dance, haven't I? Old Lee hasn't bothered us, has he?"

Billy allowed as how he hadn't. Rose Ann gave a soft, self-satisfied kind of chuckle, teasing his chin with her finger.

"That's because I know how to shunt him off to one side easy as pie. There isn't a man any place I can't handle if I want to. Been handling all kinds of men since I was eleven and started to fill out up here."

She guided his hand so he could feel, then pressed herself hard to his palm. She laughed her musky laugh.

He bent his head around to take another long kiss from her open lips, trying to ignore the fact that she liked to keep reminding him of all her swains, as if she weren't sure, yet, whether he was fit to be numbered among them.

They kissed a long time in the dark. When he tried to go further with his hands and body, she pried him off with little nos and shakings of her head. The air through the open windows of the Twister smelled of the salt sea. Against the stars the silhouettes of palms went by, *flick, flick,* in silence. A droning announcer from Southeastern Traffic Central in Atlanta reported the form-up of one of those multistate traffic jams that regularly happened on holiday weekends. Then, following a station promo wishing one and all happy holidays, a choir began *Adeste Fidelis.*

Billy put disturbing thoughts out of his head. He settled down to enjoy Rose Ann's feel against his side. The buckets of the Twister were reclined to forty-five degrees, and the machine never wavered, riding the magnetized strip through the Florida dark.

"Billy?"

"Mmm?"

"Where 'bouts were you born?"

"In Ohio, I think. Someplace between Cleveland and Erie, Pennsylvania."

"Moving?"

"Why sure. My momma had a midwife from the Tollbooth clan. She came aboard and delivered me in about a half an hour."

"Weren't born in a hospital van?"

"Nope. My old man was kind of old-fashioned about such. His kin came from the south. Midwives were good enough for him, he said."

"And what are you going to do the rest of your life?"

"Oh, find a steady trade, I guess. Maybe in Uncle Sammy's repair van." He inched his head around so that, by starshine, he might see her eyes. "All depends."

"On what, Billy?"

He slid his right hand deeper to her waist, constricted his fingers. Not too much. Just enough so that she could feel his intensity. The emotion was too deep for the simple words he could muster. "Oh, gee, Rose Ann—you know."

"I don't know, Billy. I don't know much about you even after all these nights we've gone driving. You've got sort of a pretty, peaceful face, you know?"

That worried him. He covered it by snickering: "Pretty? Aw, now—"

"Underneath, there's something I like. You could grow up to be another real hard charger. Like Colonel Tal. Now there's a man."

She was testing, wasn't she? Was she telling the truth or playing games? He felt desperate, subduing his anger in his eagerness to keep her from slipping away. "Just because I don't boot around like Lee doesn't mean I can't get tough when it's time. I can, Rose Ann, you believe me."

"I believe you if you say so, Billy." She kissed him.

During the kiss he became conscious of a strange sound among the other road noises. Now and again a stopper vehicle, mostly wagons, passed on the left; Billy'd set the automatic speed mechanism at an even 60 mph. Being an old, contraband machine, the Twister hadn't been equipped with one of the devices originally. Billy had custom-installed the magnetic link and governors. He didn't use the equipment often. The Twister was for running, not cruising. But because of the low speed tonight, stopper traffic went around them. There was an unusual amount of it for three in the morning, the reason being that this was the first night of the long Christmas weekend. Billy's mind automatically sorted the various component noises. He had trouble with the new one: a low whine, behind.

He broke the kiss, adjusted the mirror, sat up from his half-reclining position to study the glassy black image.

He saw multiple headlamps weaving in and out a couple of miles back.

Rose Ann's head was tilted dreamily to the right. She watched the stick shapes of the palms pass, *flick, flick.* The southern sky was dull red with the light of the Miami meg below the horizon.

"Ever wonder what it's like to be a stopper, Billy?"

"Sometimes."

"Can't imagine for the life of me. Living in a little box

51

house and only climbing into a machine when you want to go someplace. My papa's told me the stoppers don't hardly know the clans live on the road."

"I guess the stoppers know it, but some don't believe it, and most don't think about it, is what Colonel Tal says. The government knows it and it's okay with them. I mean, it must be okay since we've got the dole once a month and the special license tags and all. Kind of makes you feel proud to be a citizen of the *extry* state."

"You mean like a state like Florida?"

"That's the way Colonel Tal puts it. All us road people are like the fifty-second state in the U.S., he says. Our land's the road, and the government doesn't mind. That seems kind of funny in a way, when you stop to think." He swallowed deep, working up his nerve to what he'd rehearsed for days in various versions, various little set speeches, all of which he now found he'd forgotten. In a rather clumsy way he insinuated his fingers under her right arm so he could touch her breast. His loins heated.

"I don't much care one way or another about that kind of stuff, Rose Ann. I got other things perking in my mind right now."

She leaned down to kiss his hand on her breast. "Like what?"

"Whether I'm going to have the woman I want the rest of my days."

"You mean get married to her?"

Another deep, anguished swallow; all his little practiced speeches came out jumbled into, "Yes, that's what I mean."

"You mean me?"

"I do mean you, Rose Ann. I'm so crazy in love—"

He couldn't continue, bending instead to take her mouth, let her feel his intensity by the way he kissed and held her.

She wriggled her left hip tight against his. She moaned, then moaned again, raising her upper body so her breast rubbed his hand. Even while he kissed her, his mind went rocketing off every which way: was she saying yes? Was she saying no? God, how could a single, ordinary girl built like millions of other ordinary girls knot him so bad?

52

He inhaled the lilacs of the scent she always wore, kissed her hard, held her hard, harder—

A keening whine, rising steadily for the past minutes, blasted his eardrums from the left. He broke the embrace, pulled around to stare out the left window. A hood-mounted spotlight on the machine racing along beside him opened its lens to dazzle white light over them both.

Rose Ann's smeared mouth opened. Her green eyes were quickly fearful.

The spot blinked out. The turbine accelerated, went racing on up the highway trailing its whine. Billy disengaged from Rose Ann. He leaned back in his bucket, sweating and sucking hot tropical air.

The red tails of the low, mean turbine pinpointed down to nothing. Billy watched them, never took his eyes away. Rose Ann's fingers wrapped around his and clutched. She was afraid too.

That had been a Ramp machine. There was no doubt in his mind.

Werty Ramp found Billy Christmas night, in a two-by-four saloon on an upper level of one of the service vans.

There was little room in the pocket bar for anything more than the three-stool bar itself, a single table, two chairs, and a minijuke that played mountainpop in the gloom. The proprietor of the room, a fairly good looking, middle-aged bachelor named Nick Spoiler, was off in his living quarters adjoining, having sold his only customer, Billy, a pint of Lightnin'.

The minijuke scraped and squealed a succession of ballads about jealous love; somehow Billy's fingers had just gravitated to punch up tunes of that type. He was more than a little drunk when he glanced up and saw heavy-bellied, saw-legged Werty standing beside the table.

"Have a Christmas drink?" Billy offered.

"Not with you. I got a message from Lee."

"Let him bring his own goddamn messages."

"He's 'fraid that if he did that, he'd kill you on the spot."

Billy tossed off a jigger to show his contempt. He kicked a chair back. Dark-eyed, unkempt, Werty made no move to sit. He took hold of the back of the chair. "How dumb do you think ole Lee is, anyway? You been fooling with his girlfriend."

"She's not much of a girlfriend if he tools off to the Keys and heaves her beh—"

"He just wanted you to trap yourself good, Mr. Billy Spoiler," Werty said with a mean grin. "We been keepin' a nice log on every time you took her out driving in that mother of yours. It was me tailing you the other night. The camera in the spot took a nice view of you and Rose Ann hugging each other. Lee took one look and said he was calling you out. That's why I'm here."

"That's the message?"

"You got it," Werty nodded. "Just you and him, two machines, the course to be decided on. Find yourself a second. But first of all you got to say yes. Unless of course you want some of us Ramps to come around and just plain kill you."

"If that son of a bitch has hurt her—" Billy began, half rising.

Quietly, Nick Spoiler slipped in behind the back bar. He leaned on the plastowood, head cocked, frowning. Werty Ramp wigwagged his head no. "Lee's a hard charger," he said, "but not against women. You're the one he wants. You're the one beatin' his time."

Billy clenched his hand around the Lightnin' flask. "A race, you say."

"Course to be figured out by the seconds."

"What kind of race?"

"Speed and distance run. The one who clears the finish first has a clear track with Rose Ann."

Billy swallowed again. "When?"

"Soon as the holiday's over." Werty's eyes glistened in the soft reflections from the little backbar. "Lee would do it today, he's that mad. We told him it had to be done right. When he simmered down, he said okay. The way it works is, you two run flat out, and the loser on his honor leaves Rose Ann alone forever. Lee's waiting for your answer."

Desperately, Billy tried to think of a way to evade. There was none. He cursed himself silently a minute for being so careless as to get caught. Why was he so damn in love with a woman who had to be fought over? Who *loved* being fought over?

"Come on, Billy. Is it yes or no?"

Billy remembered the Superstack, and his hatred.

"Yes."

"What'll you drive?"

"The Twister, probably."

"Lee's gonna use his regular turbine. He said to tell you he'll take you no matter what kind of wheels you push."

"I know he thinks that."

"He knows that, old Spoiler sport," Werty chuckled, helping himself to the bottle of Lightnin' without so much as a by-your-leave. "I'll carry the word." He started out, then swung back. "What a goddam simple jerk you are, Spoiler, futzing round with Lee Ramp after he beat you once. Guess some folks have to be whiplashed 'fore they learn." Thrusting his hands in his pockets and grinning, Werty left.

Why should I be afraid of him? Billy wondered, his confidence helped along by another swig. *Lee's tough, he's tricky, but I got something better on my side.* He recollected Rose Ann's beautiful green-eyed face; it flamed like a holy image in a church. He felt better; afraid and better, all at once.

Funny, the terrible twists love got you into. But he did want Rose Ann, permanent, for his woman—

Didn't he?

He wanted her.

I've got a big tally to square, he thought, rising, stumbling, clutching a chair for support. The service van took a curve. The world tilted, minijuke lights smearing across Billy's vision. Then his eyes cleared. To Nick, still elbowing the bar, he said, "Guess you heard all that."

"Damned if I didn't. It's gonna be one rough run. That ole Lee is—"

"I know all about that Lee. You find me a second, okay? Real fast, would you? You find me Colonel Tal as quick as you can."

Billy's eyes glittered. Nick took just one look.

"Yes, sir, Billy, right away," he said, ducking under the bar and out the door at the run.

Uncle Sammy Spoiler stuck his head in the open right window of the Twister. "We got the dragging ramps down, Billy. You can peel off anytime."

Billy nodded. He clutched, went into reverse gear, began to back the mother along the tracks toward the rear of the service van. Around his car he saw faces, little more than blurs. Spoilers, come to wish him well. They all looked tense. He kept backing.

A dry taste fuzzed his mouth. Of a sudden, someone yelled for him to hold it. He braked with a violent kicking motion.

The Twister rocked. Damn! Showed just how gritty his nerves were, that rocking.

A face filled his open left window, green eyes wide. "Oh, Billy, I'm so glad I caught you. I had to sneak away from poppa with a lot of lies. But I had to come—" She seized his face in both hands, kissed him, deeply.

He felt her shaking. He slid his hands up around her head to hold her taffy hair. But not for long; she broke from him. The color was high in her cheeks.

"They've come in from just miles away, Billy—you've never *seen* so many vans cruising together. There's never been a run like this, has there?"

"Never a run over you," he answered, forcing a smile.

"Over me. God in heaven, it's just too much!"

"How many are out there?" he asked.

"Can't tell for sure. But poppa told me there were vans strung out from the Indiana line all the way round up past the Milwaukee meg. And you running so early at night— that makes the excitement double!"

She touched his cheek again, cool fire. She bent into the window.

"You be careful, now. You drive hard for me, will you? Here—"

She fumbled with a strip of something looped in the belt of her jumper. Billy's belly went tight; those godawful, mixed-up emotions were dogging him again. He didn't like the shine of her face, a shine that came from realizing she was the prize a man might die for tonight. But he couldn't help loving her, and his heart leaped because she'd come to wish him the luck of the run. Him, not Lee Ramp. He saw the strip she held in her hands. White. Lacy. She reached inside the Twister and began to tie the strip around his left upper arm.

"I tore this off what I wear closest to me, Billy. Closest of all. You take it along to remind you."

A chilly sexual thrill tingled his whole body as she tightened the strip of white-and-lace with a final knot. He said, "Rose Ann—you know what I'll be after if I win the run."

She fixed him with those green eyes. "Yes, I think I do."

"You. For my woman."

"Yes, Billy, I know that."

"For good and permanent."

"I know all the rules of the run, Billy," she told him in a low voice. She held his cheek again. "I've had enough of that old Lee bullyragging me. Dragging me around like his property. Why do you think I lied to poppa and sneaked off in his electric? I've never felt a thing like this before, not for any man. Billy—*win.*"

Her open mouth came down again. Her hands hugged the back of his neck. In the van's gloom, several Spoilers cracked crude jokes. A couple applauded.

"Hey, Billy," one of the Spoilers called. "Eudora says the Ramps are bellyachin' from the state line. They want to know where you are. Sun's been down half an hour."

Quickly, he touched her breast. She leaned into his fingers a moment, then drew back, giving a little, almost girlish wave. He clutched, began to back up again.

Is this right? he thought. *Do I want her? Is she just all heated up because two men are fighting for her? Would she last as my woman? Or does she just like playing one off against—?*

Doubts had to go; the rear end of the Twister lurched down. He clutched to neutral.

The reversed grabbers on the dragging ramps seized the orange mother and began to roll it backwards down the ramps. Billy concentrated on holding the wheel in line.

The rear tires left the ramps. The service van begin to accelerate. The front tires bumped onto the concrete. As the service van pulled away, Billy went through the synchromesh to forward low, then into the higher gears, picking up speed and moving into the next lane left to pass the service van.

The dragging ramps were retracting. Rose Ann waved from the van's open doors. Billy stuck his arm out the left window, waved back. The lacy piece of undergarment snapped and fluttered in the wind.

He drove easily, coolly, through the ten or eleven miles to the state line. He passed many a residence van, people crowded on the little porches, watching him. Some preferred to see the start of a run. Others would be waiting along the course that wound around the southern end of Lake Michigan past the Chicago-Milwaukee supermeg.

The wind lashing into the open machine was sharp but not cold; a late January warming spell had set in. The fields on either hand were muddy, the most recent snow melted. The west glowed like a steel furnace, sundown shining behind the polluted clouds. The pall was visible for a hundred miles.

He felt a little edgy about pushing his Twister at this early hour of the evening. But the Ramps had insisted on the time. Couldn't do much about it now.

An over-the-highway sign told him the Ohio-Indiana border was two miles away. Suddenly another mother cut into his lane half a mile ahead. Its tails flashed three times.

Billy flashed his heads in reply. He kept his distance, letting Colonel Tal's purple-flake mother lead him. Soon he spotted two turbines ahead, one running behind the other. Before long, Colonel Tal's mother overtook the first turbine. Billy accelerated till he was running beside the second. He glanced over, but twilight was settling too fast; all he saw of Lee Ramp was a silhouette. His palms sweated.

Running two each in adjoining lanes, the four machines streaked by van after van of clan people come to see the start. A steel arch loomed above the superhighway:

The moment the pace cars flashed under the arch, each one veered off into the next lane on the left or right. Billy tightened up his grip on the wheel. Lee's turbine screamed along hub to hub. They flashed under the arch, running.

Billy shoved his boot down on the accelerator, pulled ahead of the turbine by half a mile, then stayed there.

Thirty miles went by.

The bungalows of stoppers who commuted to the Chicago meg filled the scraped, treeless land on either side of the freeway. Billy threaded through a tangle of airlift shippers, checked his specially installed dash chron. Only a quarter past seven. Regular traffic, most of it freight cargo vehicles, was still heavy. There were enough stopper vehicles on the road to make it a challenge to weave in and out while maintaining constant speed and lead.

He checked his speedo. An even 88 mph. He wondered why Lee Ramp's turbine kept lying back. Lee could certainly match his pace. What were his tactics? Billy got worried.

Then he touched the lacy riband tied to his left arm. His fingers actually tingled. He began to feel a kind of divine madness. Of course he'd be first to the finish line north of the Milwaukee meg. Then he'd return, claim Rose Ann, and—

But why wasn't Lee challenging him harder? Why did the low, mean turbine's headlamps remain way back, threading through traffic while keeping a constant distance between itself and Billy's machine?

They approached the South Bend Stack, roared through. The eight westbound lanes began to curve leftward, then leftward again, swinging around the perimeter of the Chicago meg. Its satellite cities filled the sky with a maroon glow diffused through clouds of pollutants. A sulphur smell rode the wind. Private stopper vehicles became more numerous; around the biggest megs, someone was always going someplace.

Why didn't Lee Ramp make a move?

The actual driving didn't tense Billy hardly at all. It was too easy. For that reason he began to suspect it. He sweated steadily.

He flashed past van after van. The porches were jammed. People waved. The eight lanes westward became twelve. The highway, raised on piers above the stopper homes crowded on tiny plots, twisted into its big bending curve around the southern end of the lake. Streetlamps in the residential areas below the highway shrunk to fairy lights; the houses dwindled to doll dwellings. The night, the land, twinkled from horizon to horizon. The maroon pall hung over everything.

A turbine marked colorfully with stars and stripes whipped through Billy's vision way out on his left, going east. Federal Highway Patrol. Were they out heavy tonight? He didn't want to be slowed down now. He'd begun to feel the cool, liquorish taste of a win. For some reason or other, old Lee Ramp wasn't moving up at all. Trouble with his turbine plant, maybe? Billy didn't know. But he got the taste of victory all the same. He began to hum *In the Garden.*

Now exit and entrance ramps appeared about every half mile. The twelve lanes here edged the perimeter of the tightest-packed part of the meg. On his right Billy noticed that the glow had changed from maroon to orange. Billions of city lights blazed in the haze.

The little red bulb on his radiophone began to blink. He activated the set: "I hear you."

"How's your fuel, Billy?"

He consulted the gauge next to the speedo. "Down under a quarter."

"We'll pick you up at the Division exit."

"Right." He sounded almost merry as he snapped off the connection.

The superhighway was angling northwest. Soon it straightened in a more definitely northern direction, roughly parallel to the Lake Michigan shoreline and thirty miles west. Overhead signs began to post the distance to the Wisconsin line, which was also the south boundary of the Milwaukee meg. Billy threaded in and out through

60

traffic, checking and re-checking Lee Ramp's position. It never varied.

Why?

Billy began checking the giant reflective boards announcing the various cross-expressways that carried traffic into the Chicago meg. As soon as he passed under the one that said DIVISION 2 MILES he began to slack his speed. 85 mph. 80. 75. He was down to 60 mph by the time he hit the place where the Division off ramps separated from the main road.

A Spoiler electric entered from the on ramp. Billy lane-changed, moving right two lanes. The electric shifted three lanes to the left, jockeyed till it was running side by side with the orange Twister. Billy threw a series of controls. An automatic field mechanism took over, governing the speed of both vehicles. They maintained identical speeds perfectly.

Billy wiped his wet hands on the thighs of his trousers, then flicked another control that opened his gas intake on the left rear fender. All of the electric's back end had been ripped out to allow for installation of refueling equipment. In the electric's front seat, a Spoiler named Calvin gave Billy a cheery thumbs-up.

A port in the electric's rear deck opened. A stiff probe shot out across the couple of feet separating the vehicles and mated with the intake opening. An indicator on Billy's dash began to pulse, showing fuel being metered in.

He watched the fuel level rise on the indicator. All at once lights in his rear mirror distracted him. They were moving up fast. Billy stifled a yell, acted out of instinct: he smacked off the control that regulated his speed just as Lee Ramp's turbine roared up behind the fueling electric.

Lee's turbine smacked the rear of the electric hard, dropped back, screamed out and around to safety. Billy had one surreal glimpse of the extra-heavy bumperknockers mounted on the turbine's front end. And now he knew the strategy: Lee's lower rate of fuel consumption meant no on-highway fueling. But he would know Billy would have to gas up during the run. That was why he'd lain back, waiting—

Crashed from behind, the fueling electric couldn't get under control. It veered over and banged Billy's front end. Billy steered desperately to the right, swerving in ahead of an airvan coming up fast in the lane into which he turned.

The fuel probe snapped at the point where it was connected to Billy's intake. The night smelled of racing gas as the probe tube whiplashed wildly, still pumping fuel onto the highway. The airvan's horns blared. Billy whipped back into the next lane on the right, got out of the van's way just in time. He felt his tires slip.

Calvin Spoiler was frantically trying to bring his machine under control. In the lane beyond, Lee Ramp's turbine sped ahead. The electric dropped behind suddenly. Billy's back tires kept wanting to fishtail one way, then another. He held his teeth tight together, fighting the finicky power steering without much luck. Why in Christ was he so wobbly in the rear end? Why did it feel as though he were driving on jelly?

Then he realized. The snapped probe nozzle must still be jammed in his intake; the intake cover couldn't close. Racing gas was sloshing out of his own tank, slicking the rear tire on that side.

And ahead, Lee Ramp's turbine was pulling away toward Wisconsin.

Something maniacal came over Billy then. He locked on a wheelgrip that hurt his fingers, poured gas to the mother's engine with his boot sole pressing the pedal all the way to the floor. He flashed around a runabout whose driver gave him a terror-stricken look. Billy ignored the vibrations in the mother's frame, fought the touchiness of the power steering, moving up faster, pushing to the maximum until he was half a mile behind Lee Ramp's low, fleeting turbine.

Then a quarter mile.

Running two lanes left of Lee, Billy began to curse the mill of his Twister, urging greater speed as though it were a sensing, animate thing that could listen and respond. He edged up. Closer. Lee looked back over his left shoulder. His mouth dropped open—

Billy floored the pedal and cut right in a burst of new speed. He cut directly in front of Lee's machine.

For one blinding instant Billy thought he wouldn't be fast enough driving on the right oblique across Lee's path; surely he'd be broadsided, spun over, killed—a quick scarlet vision of the Firebird flashed in his head. Then he was by.

And Lee Ramp was driving through the slick of racing gas that Billy's open tank had laid down as he crossed the lane.

The turbine's tires sprayed up gas on either side. Billy pulled his Twister back onto a more or less straight course in an open lane. He checked the rear mirror. His mouth cracked a smile.

Into the gas slick before he knew it, Lee Ramp couldn't control his machine. It veered to the right, fast, straight, aimed for the outside rail. At the last moment Lee tried to correct, straighten out, but he was only half successful. He caromed the rail, shot away, braking furiously. The last Billy saw, Lee's turbine was spewing smoke from its tires as it banged the rail again and flipped. Flames erupted—

A great bend in the highway hid the rest.

Shock poured over Billy in a minute; wave after trembling wave. He checked his speedo, eased off to 75 mph. It had all happened so quickly. He'd used dirty tactics. But only after Lee Ramp had done the same. He was shaken by a mixture of delight and dread.

The radiophone blinked its red eye. With a shaking hand Billy activated it to hear:

"—onny Ray Spoiler. Billy, you making it?"

"I'm making it, Donny Ray." Donny Ray was the driver of the Spoiler health club van waiting north of the Milwaukee meg to receive and hide his mother. "Ramp's out."

"Don't we know it. Everybody's seen it."

"Everybody?" was Billy's dull response. "I didn't see—"

"You passed them all so quick you probably didn't know they were there in their machines, watching. Tollbooths, Rollbars—there's so much traffic on the bands I can't keep track of it all."

"Lee spun out. I had to dirty him—"

"He dirtied you first, I hear. Hit Calvin in the electric. That's not why I called you. There's—"

"Is he alive?" Billy interrupted. "After his turbine went over I lost track of him."

"Burned like a fireball," Donny Ray said. "We've got one report says he crawled out all bloody just before she went up. Another report says he didn't."

Billy's tired, sweating face grew ugly as the smile came back, "So he stopped?"

"Listen, let me talk a minute." The urgency jarred Billy out of his revengeful reverie. "An air shipper almost ran you down—"

He recalled blatting horns. "I got out of his way in time."

"Yeh, but he called the Patrol. Reported a wild mother on the loose. You better pour it on hard and get up here and hide, because the van driver may have got a look at your Tin. If he did, we'll have the Patrol huntin' for you in every Spoiler van from here to the Mississippi River."

That news took the keen edge off Billy's triumph. He wiped his eyes, concentrated on the unreeling lane ahead, asked a final question, "Is Calvin all right, Donny Ray?"

"The fuel car's knocked to Jesus. But he's fine."

"Glad." Billy swallowed. "Okay, I'm coming in."

As he drove on north he began to watch for machines decorated with stars and stripes. The minutes grew heavy and long. At the Illinois-Wisconsin border, he passed any number of clan vans rolling at slower speed, timing themselves to be on the scene for the victor's arrival. On the little porches, people waved handkerchiefs and held up fists. Billy barely heard the cheering that was blown around, then whipped away by wind.

It seemed to take forever to thread through the night traffic on the western fringe of the Milwaukee meg. At last the twinkling lights of stopper homes began to thin a little. Ahead, he saw the health club van with its rear doors open and its dragging ramps down.

He climbed aboard the grabbers, was pulled up and parked behind two other mothers under the false floor of the basketball court. The van doors hissed, clanged shut. He sat there in the dark, too shaken to have much reaction to the realization that he'd crossed the line first—and won Rose Ann.

It still rankled him that he'd resorted to dirty tactics. No one would hold him guilty, of course. Lee made the first dirty move.

Was Lee dead? The question pounded him with a dull terror. Boots banged on the catwalks above. He heard a ripple of voices. His right hand shook as he reached across to touch the white-and-lace hanging limp from his upper left arm.

He caressed the scrap a little; the right hand grew steadier. Faces, big white smiles, bleared around the mother as he climbed out to accept the yells and backslaps and all the hoarse cheers. He was soaking out his exhaustion in the shower room on the van's upper level when the Federal Highway Patrol officers arrived.

Old Mose Spoiler was gut-heavy, toothless, and arthritic. But Mose had a devil's twinkling eye. Mose summoned him.

Billy combed his hair, went down a hall, through double doors at one end of the basketball court.

Only three lights had been left on above the half-size court. The nearest shone on a basket and cast a webbed pool on the highly waxed wood beneath. The two Patrol officers waited in the light.

One officer was burly and black, with a young, open face. The other, taller, thinner, had a certain air of sourness. Both their uniforms were smart, though. Dacroprest, with flared lapels and Federal shoulder patches echoing the stars and stripes motif of their machines. Both wore holstered guns which Billy presumed carried the customary tranquilizing shots.

Billy caught himself hesitating, forced himself to maintain his stride. Behind him, shuffling along in bedroom slippers, old Mose laid a hand on his shoulder. Billy was even glad for the old man's bad breath.

The black Patrol officer touched his hat with one of his gauntlets. His small-eyed partner clearly didn't like that courtesy, perfunctory as it was. Old Mose shuffled up beside Billy, laid a not quite straight right arm over his shoulder, glared with wet bird eyes.

"Special Officer Claymore," said the big black. "This is Special Officer Tepper."

Claymore reached under his blouse, took hold of something with a crinkly sound. Billy felt all tied together inside. He hoped it didn't show.

"You are Billy L. Spoiler, is that right?"

"That's right."

"Owner and operator of a machine powered by illegal internal combustion, not equipped with the required anti-pollutant devices"—*Crinkle,* out came the paper; it looked like a will Billy'd seen once. It had a blue cover and was printed up inside with the odd characters found on government dole checks—"and carrying Road plate number fourteen B double 2?"

Oh God, forgive me, thought Billy, replying, "No, sir, I am not. I never heard of such a machine."

Special Officer Tepper looked more and more sour. "We'll identify him by his prints. They'll be all over the crate."

Old Mose picked a thread of slaver from the corner of his creased mouth. "You figure that kind of machine is around here, do you?"

"Yes, sir, we do," the black told him. "It was tracked electronically. This information"—rattle of document—"comes straight from the Traffic Central computers. Actually"—he slitted his eyes a little—"the Road plates with this number are supposed to be registered to a General Ford Motors Sabre Electric Runabout, so that's another illegality to contend with. You see, Mr. Spoiler, this particular plate was observed south of here tonight. But on an i.c. underhood job. Don't you people call them mothers?"

Billy rebuffed the gentle smile. "So I heard." Ah, the Tin, the Tin. Older hard chargers always said it was dangerous to show it. But those same hard chargers carried plates on their mothers nonetheless. A badge of honor;

66

a stamp of yellow, running without any Tin at all. Billy's biggest mistake had been to run the Twister at a time other than late at night.

Too late to fret over that, though. He'd agreed to the terms. And a lot of folks besides Rose Ann had commented that running while there were still plenty of stoppers on the road lent an extra dash of danger.

"Where's your Sabre, then?" Special Officer Tepper demanded all at once.

"Sold it. Down in Texas, about nine months back." Billy slipped his hand into the pocket of the Dacro-prest Denim slacks one of the attendants in the van had loaned him. Both shirt and pants fit tolerably well. He crimped his fingers around the scrap of Rose Ann's white-and-lace, fingering it in the secret of his pocket, feeling better, more comfortable in the lies every moment. Billy had a prize to lie for now—Jesus on Calvary, didn't he!

Billy figured Special Officer Tepper must have had a bad dinner, or a bad go with his gash, or both, because he wasn't giving up. "If you sold the machine, let's see the bill of sale."

"Don't have it any more," Billy said. "Believe I threw it away. Didn't know there's a law said I couldn't."

"Isn't," Claymore informed him. "But listen—let's be reasonable. Cooperate with us. It'll go easier with you when we find the machine, which was definitely observed earlier tonight—"

"With you driving, probably," Tepper said. "Admit it."

Stunned by the accusing gloved finger, Billy couldn't reply right off. Old Mose Spoiler wasn't so fearful. "He ain't admitting any such matter. He was here all night. He an' me, we been shooting pool. Ask any of the fellers who been ridin' this here van this evening. They'll tell you."

Claymore had another one of those easy, oh-hell smiles. "Bet they will. You road people have a reputation for taking care of your own."

"And lying when it's necessary," Tepper put in. The shiny-black finger of judgment went *wag* at old Mose's crooked arm lying over Billy's shoulder. "You mean to tell me you can shoot pool with an arm like that?"

Feisty, the old gentleman leaned into, not away from, the finger. "My arthuritis ain't so bad that I can't whip your ass in eight ball or any other game you name, and if you'd care to have a demonstration of the fact—"

"Shit," Tepper waved, wearily. "These people'll do anything to protect each other."

Claymore's nod said yes, though less harshly. "We'll do best to hunt for the machine," he thought aloud.

"Not without a warrant, you don't," Mose challenged.

Special Officer Claymore leafed to the last leaf of the multipage document bound in blue. "Right here, correctly drawn and signed." His dark eyes grew opaque as he stepped in close to show the warrant. Patterns cast by light falling through the basketball hoop lay over his cheeks. Billy feared him; cordiality had fled. "We'll go over this floor. Then we'll check the one below. Nobody volunteered to show us either one when we locked on and came aboard."

"Won't find nothin' out of the ordinary downstairs," old Mose vowed.

Nothing but three contraband mothers. Billy's palm sweated in his pants pocket, turning the bit of white-and-lace soggy. But he had nothing else to hold onto, and he was afraid that now the valves were stuck for fair.

The search of the van's playing floor lasted the better part of half an hour. Tepper demanded to be shown the way to the lower level. Old Mose took charge. Billy had a strangled throat, wanted to cry out a warning, beg Mose not to do it. But the old gentleman acted almost spry as he pushed open a door and flipped a switch.

Billy stared at the jamb. He couldn't bear to watch the Federal officers tramp through the door onto the rattling catwalk. He noticed from an eye corner that they had collected a small crowd: a couple of the attendants and some good old boy Spoilers in sweat suits. Billy hadn't noticed that many clansmen about the place when he entered. But then, he hadn't been paying a lot of attention.

"—watch your step goin' down," old Mose was saying. "The boys park their machines down below when they come in for a workout or some euchre. The floor gets greasy. They track it all over them stairs, too—"

So Tepper found out, banging and cursing and nearly falling off the risers and landing on—Billy sucked a breath, eyes wide, heart thudding hard—

On an electric runabout, lime-flake color, parked just where the old orange Twister had sat!

Ahead of the lime-flake job—Billy clenched his teeth to keep from yipping—two other perfectly normal, perfectly legal personal machines.

One of the good old boys in a sweat suit gigged Billy's ribs. A second one winked. No wonder the van'd got so crowded so suddenly. Most of the boys had probably come in after the Federal officers arrived.

"Where's the machines?" Billy whispered.

"Up the line," old Mose whispered back, not turning his head an inch.

"But so fast!"

"You oughta know we kin work twice that fast when it's a case o' protectin' kin. Now shut up." Louder: "You find your way all right, officers? Nothing crooked 'bout them machines, is there?"

A sullen burst of obscene words from Special Officer Tepper drifted up along with the smell of oiled rags and turbine fuel. Old Mose began to cluck, "*Hee!*" under his breath. Finally he went, "*Hee!*" so hard that he had to cover his toothless mouth.

The crowd along the catwalk swelled by the minute. The men passed whispers of congratulations, bawdy talk about what Billy was in for now that the wedding was definite. He began to feel taller, stronger, as if this might come out fine after all; there was warmth protecting him now; the warmth of family. The smell of the clan was strong around him; strong in the odors of sweat and STP shave lotions.

Down below, Special Officer Claymore said, "Okay. I guess you're clean this trip."

"Oh, you didn't find nothin'?" old Mose asked. "Told you that you wouldn't."

"Next time we will, you can count on that," Tepper warned, stomping after his partner to the lock on the left side of the van. Billy was frankly astonished that the

69

officers gave up so easily. But he didn't question his luck too hard.

A couple of minutes later, Billy and his fellow clansmen heard the suck-and-sigh of the seals letting go. The extensors whined, pulling back into the van. Soon, above the monotone song of the van's heavy tires, a turbine blasted on. The machine shrieked away.

Old Mose ran his tongue over his gums. "*Hee!*" Then, despite his bowed-up legs, he did a sort of jig. "Gone! Slick as that! Yessir, couldn't of been slicker. Let's all go have us a snort—ain't they some stashed in one of the lockers? We got here"—withered arm around Billy's shoulder again—"a number one hard charger who just knocked the gears out of them Ramps and got himself a sweet little gal in the bargain. So let's go celebrate the weddin' and put up a toast to this young tad standin' here thinkin' about his girl with his pants full of—" Old Mose paused just long enough. "Ambition!"

The boys, young and old, went wild. They slapped Billy, tousled his hair, forced him to turn on the false modesty, the wasn't-anything disclaimers. They roughhoused him up onto their shoulders and damn near took his head off on the tops of the door openings as they bore him, amid much good natured obscenity, to the card-playing room. There they passed the plasto flasks of Kentucky.

Billy took a straight swig, another. Rose Ann's green eyes glowed in his mind. Filled the day. Filled the night. Filled him, the world, everything.

Memories of flame returned; sharp-etched images of destruction.

"Yeh, but"—he forced aside a comradely hand trying to shove the Kentucky into his mouth again—"what about Lee Ramp? Anybody hear?"

"Nothing definite," said one.

"Burned up, best guess," shouted another.

"Good riddance if he did," old Mose said. "Too bad he didn't take the rest o' them rotten Ramps with him."

Another cheer. Billy fought the generous hand no longer. He threw his head back, let them pour the Kentucky down him while his mind, half dark and wicked, half light and full of joy, thought over and over and over, *Good. Good. Good.*

In both halves.

Belcher Holiday set the wedding date for March. Rose Ann seemed pleased about it. The first time they met after the challenge running—that also being the first time since the run that Billy worked up nerve to take the Twister out—Rose Ann permitted Billy to go farther with her than he ever had before, though she still stopped him before he could do everything, promising that for as soon as they were officially joined.

After the low point of thinking himself caught by the Federal Patrol, Billy's mood had zoomed up and remained euphoric; Rose Ann didn't do anything to put a pin in that. In fact, she looked at him in a new, almost worshipful way—well, damn—she should! Hadn't he whipped Lee Ramp? Only once did she mention how the wedding would disappoint her many beaus.

February. The Spoiler vans rolled north and west, through winterlocked farmlands and over bridges above cracking ice; through blizzards and sleet storms that couldn't quell the excitement that popped and sang from van to van. A wedding was a major social festivity, like Christmastime. But it was even happier, somehow, perhaps because it was unscheduled.

When the U.S. wheelmail delivered the February dole checks from the government, Billy went from commercial van to commercial van, having the punchcard punched up to take care of what he owed and establish new balances against which he could buy. He swore that every storekeeper and his customers were half looped. Work in Uncle Sammy's service van had to be done and re-done, because the boys were always horseplaying, lobbing wrenches, squirting greaseguns at each other, fooling and laughing and hijinxing to beat the band.

As the end of February neared and the caravan plowed on through a white melt under sharp days of sun, vans of other invited clans began to attach themselves, swelling the long, long train. Billy was only half conscious of this; he was busy attending to practical matters: buying a new, even more expensive Dacro-prest wedding suit; renting a family turbine wagon with built-in sleeper, for the honeymoon; acquiring a cramped efficiency in one of the family vans; cleaning out his bachelor digs and neatly packing his belongings in one of two categories: the larger would await his return from the honeymoon; the smaller would be taken on that magic drive on which he and Rose Ann —he and Rose Ann—

Just thinking of it swelled him with heat and near-tears.

Though he was busy, he did find time to inquire often about Lee Ramp. That unsettled matter troubled him; indeed, nothing else troubled him *but* that.

No one had any information, though. Even Colonel Tal, usually full of stories, rumors, speculations, wasn't much help, largely because he was already on a bleary bender in preparation for the wedding:

"Nobody's seen Lee, nobody's heard a word about Lee, so maybe he's burned up in hell where he belongs. The Ramps all scattered after the race—got their balls kicked for once. Somebody said a few of 'em was traveling in Arkansas. But it wasn't a very big batch, is the account I got. They're split up, hurting, and who cares? It serves them right. Billy, would you happen to have another flask on you?"

With brilliant sun and geese returning north along the flyways above the hushed Dakotas, the monumental day arrived.

"—pronounce you man and wife."

Reverend Cleatus Cloverleaf spread his hands above the heads of the trembling couple.

"Go on, son," whispered the divine. "Kiss her—it's legal now."

Colonel Tal, reeling unsteadily in his position as best man, hiccoughed. Down in the second row of the specially set up chairs, Belcher Holiday, giver of the bride, let out a rumble almost as loud as Tal's. Billy turned to the vision behind the film of white net. He lifted the net, fearful that the vision would suddenly vanish, pop. He was so afraid that he hesitated, slow to lean into the kiss, even as he drowned in her sweet lilac smell.

72

"Oh," Rose Ann whispered, "*Billy*—"

She cupped her hands on both sides of his mouth to hide the kiss, opening her mouth just enough to offer him a foretaste. He felt her belly, all satin-white, press his for an instant. He thought he would die, or she would faint, or both. The electronic organ pealed.

Skullpopping punch had Billy dizzy and dancing his fool head off inside of half an hour. Dressed in their clothes for travel, done with the ritual of swallowing the soggy, sugar-thick cake, he and Rose Ann romped round the floor while the guests hollered and clapped. The organ and traps ripped out some religio-rock; the noise reverberated from the walls of the four vans locked together to form the reception hall.

Billy danced and spun, clumsiness washed away by the boozy punch. He didn't care about his feet or his hands; just wanted to yell and continue this complete freedom forever.

"Oh, Billy—" Rose Ann went past, around him, a beautiful blur. "I'm so happy today."

"Are you?" he shouted over the rhythm. "Truly?"

"I am. Oh yes, Billy, I am, so very—"

Down at the end of the hall, a woman screamed.

In the sudden stillness, everyone stopped the merrymaking, though some more slowly than others. The traps banged on till a man growled, "*Ssssh!*" Rose Ann stared over Billy's shoulder, though at what, he couldn't imagine. From her expression—hell.

He turned, couldn't believe for a minute that he was seeing what he saw.

Wearing his old velveteen party coat with the black edged lapels, and his bleached-out 'tans and his heavy road boots, there stood Lee Ramp.

He kept his left hand in his party coat pocket as he started forward. Thunderstruck, Billy realized that Lee's left leg was a good three inches shorter than his right. Under his left cuff, a shiny silver brace flashed.

Rose Ann put her hand to her mouth. The left side of

Lee's face had a slit for an eye; scar tissue from hairline to chin.

"I come to kiss the bride," he said, grinning. He took his hand from his pocket. And another woman screamed and fainted.

The hand, tiny, had a glove on it. Lee peeled this off, stuffed it away. The exposed hand wasn't much more than a chunk of scar tissue, with red nubs where fingers and thumb would have been.

Lee came on, shuffling. Rose Ann made faint whimpering noises.

The first capable of moving was her father, Belcher, who threw his bulk in front of his girl. He flung both his hands out, a barrier. There was fear in his eyes. But he spoke anyway: "Don't you touch her. Don't you come one step nearer."

Jobe Spoiler, Colonel Tal, Uncle Sammy, a lot of the other Spoilers jumped in quickly and formed up behind Billy, a small army prepared for serious trouble. Last to arrive was Donny Ray; Billy heard the message he brought and passed up to the front of the crowd:

"He didn't bring no one else—"

"There's just one Ramp turbine locked on outside."

"All alone—just him."

"Not dead after all."

"Not dead."

Lee Ramp brushed at his sandy hair with the ruined hand. He grinned, an awful sight. He looked square at Billy, square and deep and long. He said to Belcher, "Okay, whatever you say. It's really him I want. I come three hundred miles since sunrise, Billy Spoiler. I can't drive so good on account of what you did. But I wanted to tell you something before you take that little whore—"

A ripple of astonishment, anger, round the hall. But no one moved. Not even Belcher. Lee didn't stop:

"—wherever you two are going. You enjoy it, y'hear? You enjoy it real good while you can. There isn't a part of this here country I can't go to, now that I'm learning to drive again. You have a right nice honeymoon, Billy Spoiler, but in between the kissing and the hugging and the—"

"Shut your filthy mouth!" thundered Reverend Cleatus Cloverleaf. "You will not use that type of language here."

Lee's sly, sidewise glance didn't seem too excited. Not angry, even; not in the least. His eyes slid back to Billy as he said, "You just remember—you'll be hearing from me."

He turned and dragged himself out. No one moved.

In a minute, a turbine turned on, screamed away. No one moved.

Reverend Cloverleaf said, "Everyone?" He stopped. No one moved.

The party was ruined.

ii / Through The Gears

"Wheels is America. America are wheels. This is a recording, a recording, a recording, a recording—"

—WALDEN GROSSEPOYNT,
33RD PRESIDENT OF
GENERAL FORD MOTORS

About four weeks after Billy Spoiler and his bride returned from their honeymoon, the quarrels began.

The caravan was rolling through Kansas, where the early wheat was starting to show under the moon. Billy'd come home tired from Uncle Sammy's repair van. His kiss, dutifully delivered to Rose Ann's cheek, lacked ardor.

Not that he'd lost his feeling for her physically. No sir, not at all. From the start, he'd been tickled to find he had a woman who was hot and ferocious when they were together. Also, as far as he could tell, no virgin. He had never worked up enough nerve to ask her about that, though, letting his curiosity stay clamped down inside, a minor ache.

Tonight he just felt bushed out. He'd been working on a runabout belonging to one of Eudora's sons; the boy hung around, constantly combing his hair and offering useless advice. Finally Billy up and told him to accelerate. The boy grabbed a power pliers. Billy slapped the tool out of his hands. Uncle Sammy came on the run.

Billy apologized; the snotty boy was persuaded to leave. But Billy wasn't much inclined to work hard on the repairs the rest of the day. He hated to walk off the job feeling he hadn't done his best, but today, that was the way it happened. It left a bad taste.

"Did you buy some beer on your way?" Rose Ann called from the efficiency's alcove kitchen, right after Billy pecked her cheek and walked off.

"Forgot."

"Oh, we're outa beer. I told you this morning."

"I'll get some tomorrow."

He squeezed into the johnny, pulled the curtain and

washed his face hard. Then he opened the medicab for the old, tough brush he used to scrub the grease from around his fingernails. His shaving tackle fell out and hit an iridescent bottle of pink shampoo. The shampoo bottle fell on the floor. Being plasto, it bounced. But the lid had been left loose. Half the pink slop spilled across the floor of the johnny; Billy swore.

Rose Ann came to the alcove, ladle in one hand, the wrist of her other pushing back a damp strand of taffy hair. She was thinner than four weeks ago. Soft gray circles had appeared under her eyes.

Billy was on his knees, sopping up the mess with a throwaway towel. Rose Ann sucked in a breath.

"Oh, that's my best, Billy. My very best."

"Well, you should of kept the goddam lid on, then. How soon is supper?"

"You keep talkin' in that tone, there won't be any supper."

She turned with a flounce. He listened, heard her walk away barefoot, begin slamming dishware and utensils every which way as she prepared the folddown table in the main room.

Billy finished mopping up. He dropped the soggy towels into the intake, heard them whoosh off, sucked to the chemical vaporizers, big waste disposal tanks down in the belly of the van.

He returned to the main room, stood a minute by the floor-to-ceiling plasto windows that opened onto the small porch. There was just his old aluminum furniture chained down out there. They couldn't afford new, not even with their doles plus what he was credited from working for Sam. They'd bought too much other new stuff.

Sundown tinged Kansas. Far away, the tiny lights of a minor meg looked smeary beneath a hovering cloud turned red by the failing light. He had an urge to cut out and go run the Twister up the road a while.

He decided against it. Too early, for one thing; he'd had enough of that on the run with Lee Ramp. Besides, he wasn't quite mad enough.

He flopped down in the inflatable chair—that cost plenty; Godamighty, the things women could think of to

80

spend money on! He picked up the remote, flipped on the little telly screwed down into its wall bracket.

An announcer was going through a pitch to the effect that the following program was rated unsuitable for youngsters and impressionable adolescents. In a moment, nude female wrestlers came on.

Rose Ann marched over, grabbed the remote. "You aren't gonna watch that filth in my house."

"Jesus, honey, I was just lookin' to see—"

"How low-down dirty those telly people have got lately? That's the same story I always heard from my papa."

She marched over to the telly as the image disappeared to a rainbow dot. She hung the remote back on its hook. Then she turned to face him.

"You want to eat now, or you want to watch filthy naked women all night?"

Billy blinked. For the first time he noticed what she was wearing. He managed a grin.

"Appears I've got my own naked woman. But I wouldn't call her a bad word. I'd call her pretty as anything."

He started for her. She whirled, beating him to the bowls of chili and the plate of cornbread on the folddown table.

"Wondered when you'd pay a mind to this," Rose Ann told him, flicking the thigh-length hem of the little crimson see-thru housedress. "I bought it for you."

A minor alarm went off in his head as they sat. "How much did it cost?"

She told him; he about choked on the first mouthful of chili.

"Rose Ann, I thought we agreed after we bought the telly last week that that'd be it for a while. We got payments on that thing, y'know. We said—"

"I know what we *said,* Billy, but I changed my mind. You want me to sit around looking like an old grease rag? I won't. My papa always had plenty of credit on balance for nice clothes. He liked me to look nice, and I did look nice, you ask the boys I used to know."

Sourly: "I don't talk to the boys you used to know."

A vision of Lee Ramp, crippled hand, ruined face,

81

silver brace, tormented him briefly. He dug into the chili. Rose Ann kept the truce only a couple of minutes. "What are we going to do tonight, Billy?"

"Oh, watch the pictures on the telly, I guess."

"Can't we go bowling?"

"Rose Ann, we said we'd be careful of spending—"

She said a nasty word under her breath. He pretended not to hear; it shocked him; revolted him. She flung a piece of cornbread onto her plate.

"All day I fraz around, cleaning and fixing up this crummy old place, then you come home and expect me to sit around some more. And not even a beer to drink!"

"All right! I'll go pick up a twelve at the general right after we eat."

She inclined her head, pursed her heavily made-up lips. "How you goin' to do that, fly? Or hitch a ride like you do when you go to work at Sammy's?"

"Okay, goddam it, I'll take the Twister!"

"And get picked up? You said yourself a dozen times— once was plenty. You may not mind hitchin' to work, but I'm already pretty sick and tired of begging the other ladies in the van for rides to the market or a shop. I got to come and go when they do, not when I want to."

Suddenly he saw a spare, stringy person underneath all her softness; it was the person he'd glimpsed before they were married, and not liked much.

She didn't let up. "Billy, there's just one answer to all this."

"What?"

"We got to have ourselves a machine."

"Oh, Rose Ann, we can't afford—"

"Yes, a respectable machine. First time we come to a mobile showroom, we're going shopping."

Exasperated, Billy whacked his own piece of cornbread down on the plate. The huge tires of the van rumbled steadily. Outside, beneath the superhighway, dark Kansas rolled by.

"Rose Ann, I told you—we can't afford it."

Without expression she said, "Shit."

"Rose Ann, you know I hate hearing words like that from—"

"Shit, shit, shit. Anybody can afford anything on the credit."

"Sure, if they want to make payments a hundred years!"

"Old Lee, he was never so tight with—"

Billy leaped out of his chair. "You bring up that bastard once more—"

"What are you going to do about it?" she blazed back, haggard, defiant, her taffy hair all a mess, limp and darker than it used to be. "You going to beat me up? You try. You just try!"

The tension held. Billy was uncertain in his anger. Finally he sank back in the chair.

Rose Ann still didn't allow him any respite, emphasizing her remarks with a chili-covered spoon wagged back and forth. "I'll lay it out for you nice and clear, Billy Spoiler. You're not going to keep me cooped up here because you're too cheap to buy a decent machine. And I'm not going to ride in that filthy, dirty old Twister, either. We either get a machine or you don't get any more. You understand what I mean? I won't let you touch me any more—ever!"

She flung down her spoon, yanked open the floor-to-ceiling windows, went out, slammed the windows.

He watched her a while. Her hair whipped and snapped against the moving backdrop of night Kansas.

Then, with a curse, he returned to his food.

Rose Ann remained on the miniature porch the rest of the evening. She sat with her arms hugging her knees while Billy slouched in the inflatable chair, watching the nude lady wrestlers, then the first of a double feature on the underground beaver network. She was still outside when he went to bed.

He must have dozed off. The curtain rings of the alcove jingled and woke him. He rolled over, making a wooly sound in his throat. Rose Ann slid under the coverlet and pressed up close beside him, flank to flank.

She didn't have a stitch on.

Right away he woke up completely.

He wasn't chilly more than a few seconds. Then he got hotter than an overheated i.c. mill.

Come on, cut it out! he thought. *Show her who's boss!*

But he was already past the point where that was possible. He was excited; she could feel.

He slid his hand over to her stomach, then down, testing her earlier angry promise.

"Billy—"

He bent in to kiss her cheek, her ear, his voice husky. "Doesn't that feel good, honey? Doesn't it?"

"Oh yes, it sure does." Her hand stayed his suddenly. "But Billy—"

"Oh, come on, Rose Ann, come on. I'm sorry I got sore."

"Oh, I'm sorry too, honey. But what I said about a machine—I mean, I get so lonesome—I could drive myself around during the day. Shop. Get a lot more done, be a lot better wife. I could buy the groceries when there are specials, instead of just whenever we can hitch rides." The conversation was calm, even while hands fought a separate battle: his straining to move, hers holding them back. "Billy, couldn't we just find out what payments on a machine would be? That wouldn't hurt, would it?"

His head pounded. His whole body ached. "Okay, okay, sure, long as we're just looking."

With a little cry she released his hand. Then she started to moan.

Things got heated up fast. Billy remembered to remind her that she ought to take her medicine. But she was already grinding against him, her tongue all over his ear as she said, "Forget the old medicine. We're married, aren't we? Go ahead, it's time we made a baby. Billy? Billy, go ahead! *Go ahead!*"

On the sixteen-lane this side of Wichita, the Spoiler caravan met some Tollbooths aiming down from the north to the southwest. Among the Tollbooth vehicles was a large one with an electrified exterior that announced:

BIG BEN'S
FANTASTIC DEALS ON GENERAL FORD WHEELS

The caravans elected to travel alongside a couple of days, visiting. Before the first day was half over, Rose Ann radiophoned Sammy's repair van to urge Billy to be home right on time, so they could go shopping. Colonel Tal offered them a lift, picked them up after supper, wished them well in their jawboning with the salesman.

Big Ben Tollbooth, himself, wasn't on the premises. Instead, a big electrified portrait of the owner hung in the left-hand show window. Billy noticed the portrait when Tal pulled up and docked; it was one of those trick signs whose details changed as you went rolling by and your point of view changed too. One minute, Big Ben looked all business. The next he had a grin this wide, and one eye shut in a wink.

Rose Ann was all tricked out in a pretty taffeta dress. Billy had washed and cleaned up extra-carefully too. Three machines stood on the gleaming showroom floor: a large, multipassenger family wagon; a little yellow electric runabout with twinkling hubs and a lot of other chrome touches; a utility vehicle decorated with lightningbolt decals. All three carried the GFM logoplate; there weren't any other manufacturers in the U.S.

"Yessir, folks, can I be of service?"

The salesman had peeled off from a group of four lounging lynx-eyed back by the dickering booths. He was young, little more than Billy's age. But he had wise old eyes, and a high pompadour. He smelled of lots of lotion and wore snappy clothes.

"Name's Henry." He flipped out an engraved card. *Henry Tollbooth, Authorized Representative.* "Folks call me Hank." He shook hands with Billy while his eye roved to Rose Ann. His smile was for her.

"We just want to look," Billy told him.

"We want to price one," Rose Ann said. She rushed to the little yellow runabout. "Oh, Billy, isn't this the cutest?"

"No, Rose Ann. It's too duded up."

"Yes," said Henry, "this little sweetie does have a lot

85

of mighty nice touches." He stroked the three-inch trim strip around one of the windows. "Customized appearance accessory grouping, four-speaker stereoradio—"

"I see," Billy interrupted, grumpily, his eye on the window sticker price: $9,472.19, including Federal road use fees, equipped and delivered. He'd mentally budgeted no more than $6,000—$6,500 top—for an economy model. He swung back, caught Henry eyeing Rose Ann's small, high bosom. She looked flushed and delicious tonight; a lot of it was makeup. Too much to suit him. He said, "What we want to do is price one on order. Just a plain runabout. We don't need all this extra stuff on it."

Henry's face fell. "Oh. Come on back to the booth."

Rose Ann had the runabout's door open. She shut it, re-opened and shut it several more times, laughing in delight at each thick *chunk*. An overpowering new machine smell rose from the interior. The showroom lights winked off the chrome circles, squares, triangles that edged the two dozen dashboard controls. Rose Ann closed her eyes, inhaled. *"Oh!"*

"That's the new car deep dip," Henry advised. "General Ford brought it out for the first time this year. Lasts practically forever. Folks love it. Of course, you only get the ordinary dip on economy models. The smell fades in six months."

"Let's go back and figure up," Billy told the man.

But Rose Ann was already sliding into the driver's bucket, caressing the moulded steering wheel with her palms. She moved her right hand to the thick chrome gearshift column sticking up at an angle from the floor under the dash. She closed her hand around the column, moved her hand slowly up and down. She glanced at Henry. "Is the price really what it says on the sticker?"

"At Big Ben's? Little lady—never. I'd say we could fix up some mighty attractive terms for you folks. This one's a real honey on the road. I drive this model myself, personally."

Rose Ann's green eyes grew wide. "Oh, is that right?"

Billy had enough sense to know that he was whipped. He stuck his hands in his pockets, eyed the sticker, itemizing the three thousand dollars worth of extra equipment he thought they could do without. Meantime, Henry Toll-booth bent into the interior, demonstrating various controls. Rose Ann's delighted laugh tinkled every other minute. Billy knew his own choice. Make a scene, or give in with a token fight. He began to wonder why he'd ever married this girl in the first place.

Of course he knew: she was so beautiful, she tore him to pieces inside. But all the things he'd noticed in her before marriage were still there. He found it depressing.

Shouldn't of guessed it would be any different, dumbhead, he thought. He cleared his throat. "I'd still like to check a price for a stripper."

"Oh, certainly," Henry said, popping out of the interior. "But I guarantee, the extra value is worth the extra cost." He put his arm over Billy's shoulder. "Come on, let's go in the booth and sharpen the old pencil. You'll come out just fine."

As they passed around the hood, Rose Ann flashed a glance through the windshield. Billy thought, *Maybe the extra's worth it for a smile like that.* Then he noticed Henry Tollbooth smiling back. He scowled.

Half an hour later they came to terms—for the equipped yellow runabout.

Henry assured him that he'd gotten an ace-high deal, then led him to another booth where a dusty old woman presided over a computer line station. Billy sat down.

"Only take a second and we'll be all set," Henry said, rubbing his hands and grinning. "I'll be out in the showroom."

Feeling tired, Billy gave the old lady the basics, including his dole check number. She punched these up on the equipment. A few lights flashed; something buzzed. A punchcard book ejected from a slot.

He smelled her perspiration as she leaned over to flip through the thick book of paged cards.

"This here's your payment record. Ever month, this amount here will be automatically deducted from your dole balance . . ."

She went on and on. Billy wasn't interested. Not even in the numbing fact that he'd just signed on for seven years of debt. Instead, he kept turning his head to watch through the translucent partition that separated the booth from the showroom. He saw indistinct figures—Henry's, Rose Ann's—close together. He heard giggling.

He pretended he understood all the old lady had said, told her thanks, jerked the card book out of her hand and hurried out.

Rose Ann didn't see him at first. Henry Tollbooth stood near her, at one side, bending to laugh into her ear. He had hold of her elbow. Rose Ann laughed again. Henry spotted Billy, straightened, oiled his smile back in place.

"All set? If you folks will step downstairs, we'll have her prepped and gassed in no time."

Sullen-eyed, Billy nodded. He seized Rose Ann's arm and led her to the stairwell. She hissed for him to let go. He lightened the pressure, but didn't release her. She jerked free, rattled on down the stairs in her heels. He came into the ratty little waiting room to find her gazing at an old news magazine with a flashy title on the cover: *THE CHINA WAR—Where Does It Stand After 20 Years?* He grabbed the magazine and threw it on a chair.

"What did you do that for, Billy?"

" 'Cause I didn't like the way you were foolin' with that salesman."

"Fooling! He was just telling me a story."

"What story?"

She laughed. "I hate to repeat it. It's kind of naughty."

"I don't know what's come over you, Rose Ann. Lately I get the weird feeling that you don't much like being married."

"Well, those chores are a big pain. Besides, what girl wouldn't rather go hear some mountainpop and have some fun instead of watching the old telly every night?"

"But you're married."

"Don't I know it!"

"You're still carrying on and fixing yourself up like"— Billy groped, whipsawing air with one hand—"like you still had boyfriends!"

"Oh, no such thing," she retorted, reaching for the

magazine and averting her eyes. Then, with a snap, she shut the magazine and hit him with that green gaze.

"Don't you tell me I can't dress up nice if I want to. Sitting around with you all the time, I start to think I'm an old rag. Oh, don't you understand, Billy? I have to fix myself up. A woman's got to know she's pretty and special, that's just"—something elusive, almost pathetic shone in her eyes a moment—"womany."

"So you go out and flirt—make a man pay attention—and you feel good again?"

"What's wrong with that? You wouldn't want to be married to an old lady nobody ever looked at." She rose, approached him almost cautiously. She put her gloved hands up behind the back of his neck, let him feel a touch of her body. "That's all it was, Billy—just talking to the man. I can't help it if I'm pretty. I like to be pretty. I like to be pretty for you."

He suspected that, remembering her beaus and all her chatter about them. But he didn't raise the issue. He gave her a quick, rough kiss, said, "Well—talk's okay, I guess. So long as that's all." He pulled away, more bothered than he cared to admit. Evidently Rose Ann needed admiration the way some men needed Lightnin'. He better get used to it, he guessed.

With a bubbling hum, the yellow electric runabout pulled alongside the waiting room. Henry jumped out. "All yours!"

They went for a spin along the beltway encircling Wichita. On the third circuit, Billy locked on to the magnetized strip. He and Rose Ann unlatched their buckets, swung them inward so they could face each other comfortably. Rose Ann reached over to touch his hand.

"Billy?"

"Uh-huh?" He was going to admit it: he enjoyed the new machine; it was no i.c. mother. But it was smooth, twinkly, new-smelling.

"I meant to tell you at supper—"

"Tell me what?"

"My time's overdue."

He gulped, jumped two inches up from the bucket, squeezed her hand and kept squeezing. "Rose Ann, that's great. Oh, man, that's terrific, that's just the best ever." He swung his head, gray eyes reflecting the lights of Wichita. "Are you happy?"

"Oh, sure."

She turned her head away to watch traffic merging in. Then she began to pay attention to straightening ruffles and flounces on her clothing. Billy laughed; again. He couldn't contain himself. "Gonna be a girl. What'll we name it? After you! Rose Ann! Little Rose Ann."

The endless colorations of nighttime Wichita went on by, in silence.

On the westering grade up beyond Denver, Billy and Rose Ann visited a wheeldoc who operated a van office and clinic. He was a somewhat shaky but pleasant old codger, a family practice man who claimed distant relationship to the Johnson clan. He fussed a lot, and smoked one sweetish cigarette after another while he took their preliminary history. He fed that, plus their financial code information, into his little line station.

In a minute, a paper tape with pricked bumps was fed out of a box. The wheeldoc fingered the bumps. He lit another brown cigarette, brushed leafy flakes off his grayed white coat, took Rose Ann's hand.

"Since this consultation is already paid for, why don't we consult? You step right in here, missus. Won't take too long," he added for Billy's information.

In the waiting room, Billy put on the headphones, listened, dialed, dialed again. Nothing but longhair. He set the phones aside and paced.

Rose Ann didn't act especially pleased by the baby's coming. That bothered him a lot. He remembered her excitement in the dark that time. Afterward she admitted that she'd studied a little homemade chart of her periods, inspired by a talk program she'd seen on telly. She said the chart helped her know when she could get pregnant. It worked like a charm.

Now she behaved oddly about it. Almost—a troubling thought—almost the exact reaction as before and after marriage. Thrilled before. Let down after.

He felt confused. That wasn't exactly an unfamiliar condition lately.

Personally, he was elated about the child. He day-dreamed so much about little Rose Ann coming that Uncle Sammy had gotten after him, though in a genial way. Pacing while he waited, Billy imagined a tiny, wrinkly flower of a baby. He cradled his arms and gazed down at them, wonder-struck.

As a result of thinking about baby Rose Ann he was in a pretty fine mood when the wheeldoc stuck his head out and summoned him with a gesture. The doc led him down a hall at whose end an accordion door stood three-quarters closed. Through the open quarter, Billy glimpsed his wife re-arranging her dress. To his surprise, the wheel-doc guided him left, into a crowded office afloat with musty-looking folios and files.

The wheeldoc shut the door, reached for a cellopak of fresh brown cigarettes, fired one up, wedged himself in behind his tiny desk. "Thought we ought to have a little chat, Mr. Spoiler."

Billy tensed. "There isn't anything wrong, is there?"

"Nothing yet. But there could be."

"What do you mean, doc?"

"Your wife's not the strongest person in the world."

"Well, she always has been on the frail side, if that's what you mean."

"Yes, partly," the wheeldoc said, pausing for a puff. His eyes looked huge behind his high-magnification specs. "This pregnancy, frankly, will probably be a pretty deli-cate one. She could lose the baby without much trouble. If anything went wrong, it could be the only one she'll ever have."

Billy's neck prickled with terror. Perhaps the wheeldoc saw, for he leaned forward, lowering his voice:

"I checked my diagnosis with the regional computer back in Denver. My findings are right on the button—your wife could miscarry easily, with serious danger to her own health. Even to her life."

The visions of little Rose Ann crumbled away in an empty, "Oh God—"

"Please, Mr. Spoiler. I say all this not to alarm you,

but to assist you. I've already told your wife the facts. With a little luck, and plenty of consideration on your part—avoiding undue excitement; don't overtire her; no sudden shocks; I'm sure you understand—she can come to full term and deliver a healthy baby. Now here—" The crabbed hands fumbled a cassette from the pocket of the dingy coat. "This is provided as part of my fee. You keep this. Give it to the next wheeldoc she sees, in about a month. He'll check my findings before he examines her." *Tick* went a nail on the cassette. "You'll have a flock of these by the time you're finished."

Billy scratched his chin. "Is that all?"

"Well, your wife is slightly depressed, but that sometimes happens early in a pregnancy."

"What's she got to be blue about?"

"She's a pretty girl, Mr. Spoiler. Yes, sir, a real looker, if you don't mind an old fellow's compliment." Billy flushed. "She's also kind of high strung. Her reaction is perfectly natural. You haven't been married long, and marriage is a pretty big adjustment for both parties. Adding a baby right away can be a double burden. Try to make life easy for your wife, now that she's pregnant. Take her out."

Billy wanted to explain that his financial resources were already stretched practically to nonexistence. But the old wheeldoc kept lecturing away. "I get the impression that a lot of what she expected in marriage isn't there. The glamour of the wedding's worn off. You don't have anything to worry about in the sex department, though. According to her, that's satisfactory."

Billy's backbone weakened again; confusion ran rampant.

"Well, Mr. Spoiler—" The wheeldoc lit another sweet smoke from the butt of the last. He extended the cassette. "Good luck to both of you. I hope you appreciate that I wasn't trying to spread gloom. I just want to make sure everything works out for the best."

Billy took the cassette, having trouble with his eyesight for some unexplained reason. He blundered toward the door, started, swung back, paler than usual. "Doc—what's it gonna be?"

92

"Oh, didn't I mention that?"

"No, sir."

"The Ribicopf test confirms a girl."

"Gee." Billy's voice was flat, atonal. "That's wonderful."

He went out with his head down. He felt nauseous. Probably from all that sweet smoke.

"Billy?"

He watched the bare thighs on the screen, heard the gruntings, gaspings, the squeals as hair was pulled. He smelled the lilac scent Rose Ann always wore. She had a lot of it on tonight. Finally he said, "What?"

"Can't we go over to the health club van, maybe?"

"Both docs said that wouldn't be good."

"Then take me to Nick's bar for a drink."

Outside, burned brown and blazing at last light, the great Central Valley of California streamed by. Billy shook his head. "Rose Ann, I wish I could, but I told you—the dole's spent till the next check arrives."

"Then borrow!" She tore at his shoulder, white, the green of her irises standing out by contrast. "If you think I'm going to sit here every night like a person in a tomb while you take off and run that old Twister to hell and back, you're crazy."

Tightening himself for what was becoming a miserably familiar wrangle, Billy said, "Rose Ann, I went over it all before. I can't borrow, the credit machines turned me down, we are up to our limit with the runabout, that's it. The only reason I go out driving so much any more is because I can't stand to stay here and argue with you when there's no money and I can't do anything about it."

She charged for the sleeping alcove, clashed back the ring-held curtains. "Well goddamn it, you cheap thing, I'll do something about it."

"What's that mean? Is that some kind of threat?"

"You'll see." She unhooked her smock, stepped out of it, found clean panties—her belly was beginning to show a trifle—put them on. "This here's Thursday, and Thursday's for fun. I'm not going to sit around watching that filthy stuff." A raging hand flung toward the telly. "I've got a little of my own put by, and I'm gonna use it to have a good time!"

Bleached white, Billy said, "A little what? A little credit?"

"Yes, sir! Put by from my own dole check!"

He jumped up, rushed to her, grabbed her wrist. "I thought this was fifty-fifty! You been holding back on me?"

"What if I have, Mr. Cheapstuff? You let go of me or I'll kick you where it hurts."

Aghast, he did. He felt horrified by his own anger. Oh, it was turning into such a goddamn mess, all out of control, like a driverless machine running wild. Every time he tried to make the slightest accommodation, something went wrong.

He snatched down his Dacro-prest sports jack. "I hope you have fun," he shouted as he ran for the refuge of the Twister.

Rolling, he felt better.

Rolling, halfboot on the gas pedal, shifting through the gears, he no longer felt like a guy without balls; no longer felt helpless in the grip of forces he couldn't handle. Out here, weaving the eight northbound lanes with the i.c. underhood mill bubbling sweetly, he ran the show. Rose Ann could go and—do anything she damn pleased. Bleeding Jesus, had he been suckered! Suckered and hung up by a noose of taffy-colored hair.

The Twister faced competition tonight. A lot of stoppers were hurrying north on the roadway, endless eights and tens of red tail lights, warning lights, indicator lights shining and winking from the rear ends of their machines. Billy recalled the day. Thursday. The start of a weekend. He put on the radiophone, zeroed onto the Fed band and soon picked up one of Western Traffic Central's emergency situation reports:

"—at virtually a total standstill southward from a hundred miles north of Santa Barbara through Los Angeles, San Diego, and across the Mexican border to just south of Ensenada. Similar conditions prevail on the northbound supers in the same area, as well as on the San Ber-

94

doo and Joshua Tree beltways. There is backup east-ward on both routes to the Nevada state line. The jam has been in existence since shortly before three p.m. this afternoon. Latest advisories indicate that the situation is worsening hourly. Motorists whose travel is not essential are strongly urged—"

Saying a swearword, Billy flipped off.

A lot of good it did to warn the stoppers to stay home on weekends. Each stopper considered himself special, his weekend plans so important that he'd sit on his tailbone smack in the middle of a two-state, hundred-mile jam just so he could arrive at some overcrowded resort by the time the weekend was half over. Billy spit out the window into the heated August air of the Central Valley to show what he thought about that.

Then he took a swig from the Lightnin' he'd picked up at Nick Spoiler's bar before peeling off. He'd parked the yellow electric in the bay at the bottom of the van in which Nick's bar was located. He thought of Rose Ann trying to head someplace minus wheels. He laughed and swigged a second time.

Driving tonight had a savor. Already the jam was build-ing this far north; he weaved in and out among stoppers probably headed for three days of fun in the Friscobay meg.

Not that the Central Valley was exactly empty any more. On both right and left, the chain of smaller megs was practically continuous. Rows of home lights under pollutant clouds were broken only by the roofs of low mile-long enclosed farms where, Billy heard tell, produce was raised in tanks of cruddy-smelling liquid.

He couldn't help feeling slightly depressed by all the jumbly lights flicking and winking past him to either side of the northering road; more stoppers poured on at every ramp. Very soon, below the Monterey meg, average speed of all the machines on the highway began to slacken.

Billy tried to force his way through the pack, failed. He had to sit with palms tickling and an eye fixed on the speedo. It dropped from 60 mph to 55. Then to 50. The freedom of boiling along in the Twister soon lost its special joy.

Well, he should know better than to run on a weekend.

He passed a blaze of red lights, wrecking cranes, mangled steel. Eight or ten stopper machines had banged together; he was unmoved. Weekend multicar fatalities were a buck a dozen. They were caused by the ineptness of the stopper drivers.

He veered over left in front of a family wagon, just to avoid being too close to the stars-and-stripes Patrol machines stopped by the wreckage. The wagon-pusher laid on the horn. Billy gave him a finger out the side window. The wreck lights whipped on back into the blaze of headlamps behind him. Billy hummed *Sweet Hour of Prayer* in a listless way.

The rest of the night turned into a real chore. Above the Monterey cutoffs, he maneuvered over to a loopback. But southbound traffic was no better. He finished the Lightnin' too soon. Nothing remained but fighting the stoppers all the way home.

About four in the morning he passed the clan vans heading north. It took him an hour to go south, loop back again, and catch up. The jams had unclogged a little about three o'clock. The break might last till sunup. But Billy didn't find much relief in that. His throat tasted of brown from all the liquor and the fretting, and when he finally maneuvered the Twister up the dragging ramps and parked it alongside the yellow electric in the belly of the van, he wanted another jolt of popskull.

He went upstairs to Nick Spoiler's place, even though three was regular closing time. As usual, no locked doors stopped him anywhere.

The bar was empty. Billy scratched his chin, hitched up on one of the three stools, rang the bell. A small service light burned on the back bar, right below an old, heroic-looking litho of Granatelli beside one of his primitive machines. Billy glanced over past the dark minijuke to the partition separating the bar from Nick Spoiler's living quarters. He rang again.

The folding partition unlatched from inside. Nick poked his gray head through. "Listen, we're closed up, I—Billy."

The way he said it, with such an odd expression, tickled

Billy's curiosity in a chilly way. There was a strange odor in the air, too, mixed in with the smell of stale smoke.

"Just let me have a flask of Lightnin' on the tab and you can go back to bed, Nick."

"Well, I"—Nick flashed a look into a corner; why, Billy couldn't imagine. "Billy, I'm pretty damn wore out—"

"Oh, it won't kill you to walk over here and punch up a charge."

"Well, I suppose—okay."

Nick eased sideways out of the opening so as not to push the partition open any further. He wore a pair of cheap watersilk night shorts and nothing else. For a man his age, he had a hard-looking gut, Billy observed as his nose kept tickling and wrinkling. He noticed the dim glow of a bedlamp, way in back beyond the partition. What the hell was that smell?

Nick began to rummage among his stock, clacking plasto pints and fifths and knocking over a couple. Elbows on the bar, Billy rubbed his eyes. His head ached from fighting the stopper traffic.

"You must of gone to bed with a case of the meemies, Nick. You're shaking like a hood scoop that—"

"Honey?" said a drowsy voice from way back.

Billy said, "Who's that?"

"Nick lover? Where are you?"

Nick Spoiler began to back up. He couldn't go far, only to the back bar. But he kept trying. He raised his hands, palms out, like barriers.

"Listen, now, Billy. I didn't ask for it. She made the play first. She's the one who wanted to step around. Why, the first time, she damn near begged me to—"

With a scream, Billy went over the bar.

Nick yelped, dodged, ducked, scrambled out from behind the bar on all fours. Sprawled across the imitation wood, Billy heard Nick run out the door. Rose Ann was noisily rumpling covers back there. Then she got up; he could hear her footsteps. He flung open the partition just as she reached it.

Her green eyes got huge and she took a step back. "Oh Jesus on the cross—"

"How'd you get here, Rose Ann?"

She retreated to the rumpled bunk. He chased her, kicking aside an empty pint, slapping her hand when she reached to snap off the little glowlight. His hand knocked the light, too, spinning crazy shadows across the walls. She tried to burrow into the covers. He saw her privateness through a nighty he'd never seen before. The bedding reeked of perspiration and the scent he'd smelled when he walked in—her stinking lilac.

He twisted his hands in her hair.

"How'd you get here, Rose Ann?"

"—I sent him a message after you lef—"

"You and that shitty barkeep? You and him? How long, Rose Ann?"

She twisted, tried to pull away from his hands in her hair, tried to jerk the covers to her neck at the same time. Her eyes showed him real venom. "What's it to you?"

He smacked her head against the wall at the end of the bunk. "I asked you a question, you dirty little gash. How long?"

"What'd"—she was breathing hard, tears wet her cheeks suddenly—"what'd you expect me to do, you arguing all the time, and running off to roar around in that filthy old mother night after night just 'cause you couldn't stand to be around me? D' you expect me to sit and rot?"

"I asked you"—he used her hair to force her head back again, bang, hard—"how long, Rose Ann?"

"A week, two weeks, I lost count of—you let go! You're hurting—"

"A week?" Billy banged her head again. She screamed. "Two weeks? You scabby, whoring old gash—" His words grew incoherent as he banged her head a few more times, then pulled her by the hair, dragged her out of the double bunk and threw her on the floor.

Rose Ann had her elbows tight against her ribs, protecting her breasts. Her hands hid her eyes.

Billy hauled off and kicked her ribs. She spun over, arms outflung, head rolling sidewise as she gave a long, shuddery moan.

When his mind latched back into place, there was a crowd, attracted by the racket. He recognized his surroundings. Rose Ann was still lying on the floor, though somebody had draped her with a sheet from the neck down. He really woke up when Colonel Tal shouldered in from the bar with a decanter of last night's mix water and emptied it over his head.

Sputtering, defused, Billy blinked. He dropped to his knees beside his wife, touched her slowly moving breast, and right away the rage came back. "That goddamn sneaking Nick!"

Tal and others restrained him. "No use," Tal said. "Nick took off in his machine. In his shorts. We won't see him again." Suddenly Tal slapped Billy's face. "Listen, boy! You better think about that wife of yours. She's hurt."

Still not getting through, Tal shook Billy by the shoulders. "You got to do something about her, Billy. Fast."

He started to weep. "I didn't mean to bang her up. I just got so mad."

Right then he really noticed Rose Ann's waxy pallor. He knelt again, laid his cheek on her mouth. She was breathing. But that was about it. The cautions of the wheeldocs spilled through his head.

"Oh, Jesus, Rose Ann, I didn't mean—" Wildly, he began shoving his arm under her to protect her, raise her, carry her.

Colonel Tal pulled him off, then took charge of organizing things. He warned Billy that moving Rose Ann roughly at this stage could result in further harm. A couple of the men bundled her gently in a blanket. Billy couldn't stand to see her unconscious, looking so frail. He went to the barroom, found a plasto bottle of Lightnin'.

Tal jerked it out of his hands. "None of that."

"Colonel Tal, she was stepping around on me!"

"Happens plenty when young ones get all heated and hitched up without knowing what they're getting into. You save all the whys and wherefores for later."

"But I didn't mean to rough her so much. I just went crazy. Oh, God, Colonel, the wheeldocs told us—"

"Everybody in these vans knows 'xactly what the wheeldocs told you. Hell, you bragged on the whole business often enough. What you got to do—" Tal's veined old hands beat another bottle of Lightnin' out of Billy's fingers. "Will you stop? You *hurt* her. She's your *wife*. What you got to do is get her to another wheeldoc right away, so he can look her over and see if anything's wrong."

Scared, Billy raked his nails across his mouth. *Little Rose Ann,* he thought. *Baby Rose Ann—*

"There can't be anything wrong, Colonel. She'll be all right, I know she'll—"

"Stop wasting time blabbering. What's done is done. Just get busy undoing it."

"All right." Billy started past him. "A wheeldoc—"

Tal shoved him back, hard.

"Will you quit runnin' off like a brat with no god damn brains? I already sent somebody for Eudora. She'll get on the link and find the nearest wheeldoc. It's up to you to get Rose Ann there. Now where's your machine?"

"Parked downstairs."

"Which one?"

"Both." Oh, the sting of remembering now; remembering how he'd stashed the yellow electric down below, just to spite her. Oh, Jesus, how could he have done such an awful thing?

Finally he got hold of himself. He knew Colonel Tal was right. If he wanted to set things straight, it was no time for moaning and feeling sorry.

"Uh, Colonel, what?"

"I said, Billy, which car do you want to drive? I'll have the boys bundle your wife in and see she's warm."

Billy thought, with effort. When he docked at a wheeldoc's, the Twister would be conspicuous.

But the yellow runabout was too slow.

Yes, but the runabout's springing was up to snuff. The ride would be smoother.

Yes, but he couldn't maneuver it as well, or travel as fast.

Tal's eyes were fixed on him, unmercifully.

Billy said, "The Twister."

Tal started giving orders. Three of the men picked up Rose Ann's blankets, sling-fashion, and carried her carefully out of the little bar. Tal came along behind, having

100

refused Billy permission to help with the carrying. The Colonel was barefoot. His old mashed toenails were yellow, hard-looking as some kind of horn. He was wearing a patched flannelette nightshirt. They went down the iron stairs to the bowels of the van.

"Hated to rag you so hard, Billy," the older man said. "But I had to wake you up."

Billy watched the swaying figure being handled at the bottom of the stairs. Rose Ann's taffy hair hung long and loose. "I know, Colonel."

"I feel for you, boy. But this's no time for feelings. It's time for doin', understand?"

"I'll get her there," Billy said. "Do you think I don't love her? I do. I love her more than anything. I'll get her there."

"Good." The old man nodded. "Plenty of time for pointin' fingers later. Right now, the job is to see there is a later."

For a second Billy wanted to yell at the old bastard to stop being so cruel. He didn't yell. Instead, he knuckled his eyes. Lights flashed on throughout the belly of the van. The men opened the Twister's right door; the orange paint flashed hard highlights.

Tal supervised getting Rose Ann loaded just right. He had the men spread her on the rear seat, then pile blankets into the floor wells, building them up so that if she rolled forward suddenly, she wouldn't drop onto something hard. Other Spoilers got busy opening the rear doors and lowering the dragging ramps.

Hot California morning poured into the van's belly. Out on the left, in the open lanes, machines full of gawking stoppers cruised by. Traffic sounds beat on the insides of Billy's head. He started feeling queasy again.

"Hey, boys. I found one."

Heads tilted up. Eudora leaned on the catwalk rail, her hair in roller-curlers. "The nearest wheeldoc's cruising on Super-One down by Dago. He's related to the Boots clan. He'll move over to the slowest northbound in about five or six hours. He'll go north to San Clemente, then take the southbounds back to Dago. He'll keep doing that till you catch up to him. Doc Benjamin Boots. Got that, Billy?"

He nodded. "I can make Dago in a lot less'n five hours."

"Not with the jams they're reporting. It's the weekend, remember?"

Billy couldn't say a word.

Tal said, "You better roll."

Billy slid into the driver's bucket, kicked on the i.c. mill, started to back in response to the flagging of the men on either side of the top of the dragging ramps. He flipped his right arm up, across, wrenched his head around to the right in order to watch through the rear window. He saw Rose Ann.

She was barely breathing, it seemed. Just her cheeks and eyes and hair showed above the piled blankets. Under them, something tented up, fell, rose, fell again, as if she were moving a hand spasmodically. Billy's rear tires bumped up high—

"Watch your goddam drivin'!" Tal shouted.

Before the Twister ran up, over and off the raised edge of the channels that led to the back of the van, Billy went into low forward, straightened out. Then he backed again, more careful this time. His forehead dripped with a sweat that the hot morning air evaporated into chilliness.

The grabbers caught. He let himself be carried rearward and released, geared to forward, pulled into the next lane without looking.

A turbine slammed on its brakes. Billy accelerated. He heard crashings; checked the rearvision mirror.

The turbine sport model had caused an accordion-smash running back to involve eight or ten machines. Billy's face remained a blank. He booted the Twister ahead.

Don't die, he thought. *I didn't mean it. Don't die, baby Rose Ann.*

Machines. Machines everywhere. He began to fight. There was no other word for it: creeping up on a potential slot, bulling his way left, chickening out the other driver to gain the new lane, then pouring it on for maybe a

102

quarter of a mile before the bogdown started again. A couple of times stoppers made him so furious with their expressions of curiosity that he fingered them. But that didn't do much to relieve his tension.

In forty-five minutes he came to a loopback. He nearly caused another wreck merging into it. Going south, he had a clear track for about ten miles. He laced in and out at 90 mph among the stopper machines riding the magnetized strips. The California sun was big through the haze; hoods, tops, decks, fenderplates reflected and reflected like dull mirrors.

"—special alert from Western Traffic Central." Billy had tuned in the Fed band right after passing up the clan caravan. The government's noncommercial news, discussion and music programs were interrupted frequently on weekends by the dispassionate voice of the roadway situation announcer.

"The jam which reaches south from Friscobay is expected to meld with the jam reaching northward from Baja California, Mexico, through the L.A. meg, and become a single unified jam of slow to moderate speed, reaching from one hundred miles north of Friscobay to one hundred miles south of Ensenada. Latest computerized predictions look for this condition within one hour. Motorists are advised to go home, leave the highways, especially U.S. Internation Super-One, unless their trip is absolutely necessary."

Billy ticked sweat off his cheek with an index nail. The poor bum sounded tired out; why not? What driver would say his affairs weren't important? Who in this hurtling metal river? Nobody, that's who. The government knew it.

"—motorists who cannot cancel their trips are urged to use the magnetized lanes, and to proceed with extreme caution. Federally enforced limits are 80 mph for private machines, 70 mph for commercial—"

A slot. Billy went shooting up fast, kicking the accelerator so hard the Twister actually rocked. In the rear, Rose Ann moaned.

He twanged the right front fender of a light delivery job as he moved over and into the clear. He paid no mind to the enraged driver, twisting instead to look at his wife.

103

Her smeary mouth opened and shut, making a whistle of sound. She seemed to be squeezing her eyelids together.

He refocused on the road ahead none too soon, hit the brake pedal. He bulled left again; the Twister wobbled, requiring hasty correction.

Lousy, stinking power steering. No good from the beginning. Just now it had almost smashed him into the stopper on his left. He blazed out to another slot, shot up past the sedan whose tailpipe he'd almost climbed. Inside, a little old grayhaired woman hunched over the wheel, gripping it as if she were in combat. Her neck was poked forward toward the windshield. Her teeth were bared and clenched. Billy's sinuses began to hurt.

By the time he reached the Fresno off ramps, the northern and southern jams had melded together for fair. His speed fluctuated. Down to 48 mph. Up to 55 again. Then slacking off dangerously. To 43 mph.

42 mph.

Billy rode the horn, urging the motorist ahead to close up the space between himself and the next car forward. The machine ahead didn't increase its speed. Another damn pophead riding the strip! Billy banged the guy's left rear as he aced around.

He had a clear look at maybe a quarter mile of road. He ate it up in seconds, then slacked back to an uncomfortable 45. Even conscious of Rose Ann's fragile condition, he couldn't stand slowing down; he couldn't toss off the belly pains he got whenever speed threatened to fall to near 40 mph. The reactions were part of him, like breathing.

The hot, hazy sun began to slant through the Twister's right window. Past noon already? Christ on Calvary! He hadn't even hit Santa Barb yet.

But he was near; the gigantic roadspanning overheads told him. So did the stopper houses, rowed out for miles on either hand, merging one into another into the distance under the soiled clouds. The air smelled of the chemicals of the highway and other, more pungent ones besides.

Only at very infrequent times like this—running near a truly gigantic meg—did Billy turn over in his mind what

104

he knew for a fact but never much bothered about: the whole U.S. of A. was swollen almost to bursting. He recalled the Reverend Cloverleaf, at Christmas, saying it wasn't so and damning those who did say it. Apparently the Reverend never used his own good eyes when his machine took him near the largest megs.

Just look at the glinting machines lined up on the access ramps now, and receding miles into the distance. Just look at the house-boxes stacked alongside—even underneath—elevated Super-One. Even now, with his weight of anxiety, he was grateful to be free on the roads. How much fatter could it get down below? What must it be like, as a stopper, to have to come to a halt amid all that mess and crowding?

His eyes warned him. Stars and stripes flashed.

Then he saw that the turbine was on his extreme left, traveling the northbounds. The Federal Highway Patrolmen spotted him, too. But they were so glued up in their own jam, they'd never find a loopback in time to catch him.

Gradually he lost sight of the Patrol turbine. But having seen it did remind him—uncomfortably—that he was pushing an illegal mother in full daylight. What if that Patrol machine used the radiophone to set a trap for him ahead? He edged down under the wheel.

In a few minutes he checked Rose Ann again. The fishy movement of her mouth had stopped. Good. He tried to think of a hymn he liked. He couldn't recall one.

On the Fed band, some professors were blabbing about expanding the tactical options in the China war. The situation announcer broke in.

"—latest national statistics released by Traffic Central Headquarters in Washington. During the first twelve hours of the weekend, there have been one thousand, one hundred and nineteen traffic fatalities, and reported injuries totalling seven thousand, six hundred and twenty seven. This is point oh seven percent above the normal casualty rate for a three day nonholiday summer weekend, and Traffic Central computers predict that if the trend continues—"

105

"If the trend continues," Billy said, "she's gonna die or something."

The words just tore out of him; he downshifted, then shifted up again, pushing through the glare and shriek; pushing every minute.

"—motorists are advised to use extreme caution, especially throughout the eleven-state Western region, where jams of gargantuan proportions are developing due to the unusually fine weather. Unless traveling is absolutely essential, the government strongly urges that—"

"Oh, fuck you!" Billy shouted.

Then he shook his head. He rubbed his head; sinus was bothering him in earnest. He rummaged in the glove. No medicine, nothing but a mess of maps and a couple of stale Acapulco Golds. Couldn't risk a high in this traffic. But Christ, he was starving. He should have brought some food.

The sun continued to dull, casting little more than ghost-shadows on his right leg; the lower edge of the right window was a shadow-line growing ever fainter as he moved deeper into the putrid clouds over Southern California.

He passed through Santa Barbara—or rather, over its outlying edges—riding the nervous edge of 41 mph. Then things really heavied up. Ten lanes wide southbound, Super-One crawled at no more than 45 mph. It took all of Billy's gut and skill to pull out and around the slower drivers, to avoid being slowed down by the more and more frequent roadside disasters of metal and blood, pyramids of ruin pulled off, piled up, and awaiting whatever mercy could get through the crush of rushing machines.

From the back, Rose Ann let out a moan.

"Don't you worry, honey," Billy said, checking ahead. Everyone was rolling at an even 46 mph. "We're almost there."

Big fat lie. He'd been rolling since morning and he was only on the approaches to the L.A. meg. The time had already wound down to after four. He kept saying soothing things while he made sure of the situation. Yes, okay—he could turn around for a minute and look at her.

He did.

Somehow Rose Ann had gotten her head wedged beneath the right-hand rear seat armrest. Her knees poked up, pulling the blankets tight. In the general area of her midsection, the blanket had a stain.

The stain was nearly as wide as a grown man's fist. The blanket was a moldy old saddle tan, much discolored by dirt and grime. The stain looked black. It glistened.

"Oh," Billy said. "Oh God, don't let it happen to her."

A quick check of the road. He slewed off and shifted, tires yelling as he almost climbed another tail end. Three silly-ass girls laughed and waved as he cut back in ahead of them.

Then, as if it were some punishment his own mind had dreamed up—*next time you look, it'll be gone*—he craned around to look in the back again.

The stain was still there. She was bleeding.

He took more chances than ever. He kicked the Twister harder than he should, all the way up to 85 mph along sudden, unexpected half-mile open stretches, pouring on brakes to make the machine's frame shudder when he slowed down. He began to smell bad from his own perspiration as he fought mile by mile under the polluting cloud of the L.A. meg. But its rotten breath smelled worse than he did.

He angled in over Hollywood as dark came on. He galled his way through the ancient, original Stack, two of those lanes were—goddam stupidity!—shut for repairs. He was pushing south into the repetitive dreariness of upper Orange County when he noticed that the stain on Rose Ann's blanket had grown larger. It was about as wide as two fists. He began to say prayers, aloud.

A couple of minutes of that and he cut off, dialing up the radiophone volume to catch something that had snagged his attention:

"—special situation alert to motorists southbound on U.S. Internation Super-One between Greater Anaheim and the United States-Mexican border. There has been a major twenty-three machine crash in the vicinity of the San Clemente southbound ramps. Rescue vehicles cannot

107

reach the scene of the mishap unless lanes are cleared. Three lanes are blocked by a large mobile physician's van which overturned following—"

That was all Billy needed to start dialing frantically till he picked up a commercial band.

He waited in a state of controlled hysteria while three rockpop numbers wore themselves out. Then came the bulletin, recapping the government announcement, but adding the details the government net never carried: names of those who, by instantaneous computerized feed of their plate numbers to Washington, had already been reported dead to their next of kin:

"—Mrs. Emily Sockman, a housewife of Gardena; Mr. Estevan Franco, Mrs. Franco, and two unidentified children, of Ensenada, Mexico; Father Roger Willems, S.J., of Thousand Oaks; Dr. Benjamin Boots, a mobile physician whose overturned van has seriously hampered activities of medical rescue crews; Mr. and Mrs.—"

To the windshield Billy screamed, "What am I gonna do?"

A driver on his left heard him, gave him a funny stare. Billy turned like a wild man—oh Mary at the Mount, she was still bleeding; the stain was bigger than ever.

He turned front again, facing the smeared twilight, the blurred lights of the warehouses and factories of upper Orange County.

What *could* he do? Radiophone the Federal Highway Patrol? Shit, they'd probably nail him for illegal operation of a mother. They'd jail him, talk at him, and while they talked, Rose Ann could get worse.

Try to raise Eudora back at the caravan up north? Have her locate the next nearest wheeldoc? But how would he ever get there in time? Even if there was a doc as close as fifty miles, how would he ever make it?

Even before he was conscious of knowing what he had to do, he was doing it. He discovered it when a horn howled. He kept slanting to the right, to a spot that wasn't there.

The spot opened. The driver behind didn't want to be smashed. Billy straightened out.

108

He turned his head, counted over. Six lanes to go. A gigantic sparkly over-the-road zoomed up out of the murk.

ANAHEIM — DISNEY CITY
USE NEXT 3 EXITS

Billy rammed over, crossing two lanes this time.

He was out of his mind. He had to be. But what choice did he have? His head buzzed.

Choice? None.

At least, none that made sense to him with Rose Ann starting to whimper a little, and thrash from side to side under the bloody blankets.

What would they think of him? What would Colonel Tal say? But what had the Colonel said already?

What's done is done. Just get busy undoing it.

He didn't know if he had the strength; that was the real problem. Riding there in the mother, smelling the rot of evening air held down tight by the clouds of Orange County, he didn't know if he had the belly and the balls to go all the way.

He craned round for one more look at Rose Ann.

Sure he did.

He balled the Twister to the right, then to the right some more, cursing other drivers, his brown hair flying, and suddenly there he was: arrowing down the extreme right-hand lane at 55 mph. There was a lot less traffic in this lane; a commercial airvan was just pulling out of sight down on the off ramp, disappearing down among the piers, the smogbound cloverleafs that led around and around till they eventually came out on—

EXIT

He knuckled his mouth.

RAMP SPEED 45 MPH

The Twister roared off at an oblique right. The front end dipped. He was on the ramp going down.

Intersection ahead. Signs; unfamiliar town-names; arrows. Billy chose the left, the Twister's rear end slipping sideways—he was going too fast! He touched the brake for control.

He was on a downward spiral that ended somewhere below in blurred lights.

EXIT SPEED 35 MPH

His teeth were together, edge to edge. He braked, braked again. His guts began to fall out; or so it felt. But the needle came down—43, 42, 42—as he started— *Jesus save me*—stopping.

Where the turbine came from, Billy didn't know. His whole shaky concentration was on the downslope. He kept his half-boot on the gas pedal, unable as yet to bring himself to drop the mother under 40 mph.

The corkscrew straightened out. But ahead, another fork interrupted the downward route. Billy noted the sign.

WHEN RAMP'S FULL USE WAITING CIRCLE — LEFT

Glancing around, he puzzled it out in a couple seconds: the left forking led onto a big loop of concrete suspended between Super-One above and the town below. The loop allowed motorists to circle round and round while waiting for ramp traffic to clear. Radials—other ramps—merged into and off of the suspended loop.

All that understanding fought to the top of his addled head in a couple of seconds. Then his rearvision glass showed a turbine on him. The hood was decorated with stars and stripes.

About a half mile remained before he reached the spot where the ramp forked. He was still traveling at 42 mph, saying to himself, *Come on, wind her down, you made up your mind already*. The tiny red dashlight glowed suddenly, then went off.

He stared at the dashlight in a dull way. He lifted his

eyes to the rear glass again. Was one of the Federal Highway Patrolmen—the one not driving?—wigwagging him down?

The dashboard's red spot of color continued to burn, darken, slowly, dreamily. Outside, visibility grew poor; he'd descended into the upper edges of ground-level smog.

All at once the Patrol turbine turned on its roof flash, big revolving knives of red light slashing, *whick,* over the back of his mother; *whick,* across the silvered surface of the rearvision, very fast; *whick,* across the piers encircling the ramp. The Patrol let go with its howler, too.

That prodded Billy to thrust his hand to the radiophone control, fumble to the intercar wavelength. In the back, Rose Ann made a noise. He tried not to listen. A filtered voice rattled through:

"Road plate fourteen B double 2, do you hear me? Answer."

Swallowing, Billy said, "I hear you."

Oh, they had him. An arrest for pushing an illegal i.c. underhood machine at very least. He edged onto the gas pedal, shooting toward the ramp fork faster, his whole body responding to a frantic urge: *outrun them.*

"Don't try that, fourteen B double 2," said the pursuer's voice, above the howler's howling. "We can pour on twice your speed."

The fork zoomed up fast under Billy's lights; the filtered voice picked up speed too. "Take the loop. I say, circle left onto the loop. Do you read?"

Billy hung onto the wheel, still shooting forward. All of it drove into his head: whick of light; yammer of howler; strangeness of those whorled lights down at the end of the exit ramp; a foreign land where his whole sweating, itching body told him he didn't belong.

"I say," shouted the filter-voice, "circle left and—"

At the last second, Billy spun the wheel.

He wasn't even conscious of making the decision. The mother fishtailed, hurling into the loop. A moment's shame, then a deeper guilt, seized him: he was afraid of the big sleek machine swinging now to follow his tailpipe; but he was more afraid of the alien land of lights below. He didn't dare look at Rose Ann.

He checked the speedo. Barely 43 mph. It wasn't difficult to drive the loop at that speed; the concrete was gently banked, the continuous curve moderate. Lights pushed at his eyes, flashed on by. Stoppers; cruising the loop heading the other way. The filter-voice told him:

"Now lock onto the magnetic strip, fourteen B. We want to talk to you."

He cleared his throat. "I got no strip gear," he lied.

A conference at the other end of the channel; the voices were indistinct. Then: "You're Road, aren't you?"

"Yes, sir." Christ! Why'd he throw that *sir* in? It just popped out; he wiped his slick forehead. "My wife, she—"

"Where's your caravan?"

"Up north, in the Valley. Listen, officers, my wife—"

"Keep your speed where it was!"

That jolted Billy; he'd edged her up to near 50, unconsciously. The voice told him: "If you can't lock on, just keep riding the loop on around. Don't get off. Repeat —don't get off the loop."

A second, remote voice said, "Ask him why he's leaving."

Billy's sinuses throbbed. Should he have lied about the strip gear? He didn't want to get locked on, in case he had to try a fast breakaway. But what was all this about? Why did they want to play with him, fool with him, the two cars whizzing round and round with the roar of Super-One above? Why didn't they just go ahead and slap an arrest on him? *Rose Ann, I'm sorry about getting caught. Maybe they'll help if I explain.*

"Why are you leaving the highway, fourteen B?"

"I got my wife in back, officers. She's gonna have a baby but she's in trouble. She got hurt this morning, way up north in the Valley. I brought her down here to see a doc. I mean, she's really in bad shape."

"What's the matter with a wheeldoc, fourteen B?"

Encouraged—they'd switched off the howler, though the flash kept whipping scarlet over the back end of his machine—Billy said, "The one I was on the way to see down by Dago got himself killed." He went over the details, eyes on the unreeling loop; the mother passed the junction where he'd left the exit ramp. "If I don't find somebody to take care of her, officers, she might die. I figured"—he stuck his tongue out to moisten his dry lips, but there was no moisture on his tongue, either—"I figured I could find a doc or a hosp if I stopped in one of these here towns."

Another conference. A snatch of conversation: "—you better get hold of the counselor."

The counselor? Billy blinked, tight through the chest. The first Patrolman informed him, "We're putting out an automatic call for another fella. He's going to talk to you, fourteen B. He might not get here for five or ten minutes so you just cruise the loop like you are."

Suddenly Billy's dammed fear broke: "Talk to me? Why does somebody have to talk to me? If you're gonna nail me, do it, but—"

"Who said anything about nailing you, fourteen B?"

Billy was numb for a while, trying to figure out that bombshell. Around the loop they went. Around again. And one more time. Ideas, plans, tumbled through Billy's head.

Ditch them.

Fall back and wreck them.

Explain to them.

Each plan was rejected—foolish—right after he thought of it. He felt insignificant, unsure, lost. The best he could do was hang onto the wheel, fighting the touchy power steering as he rode around and around, tortured by one last question: Was he helping Rose Ann by this delay? Or killing her?

Headlights—his, the turbine's—pushed through the gently drifting smog clouds. It was this low lying murk that made traffic control by aerial vehicle, such as helicopters, virtually impossible; the only places aerial craft could operate successfully were places far away from the polluted megs—and that was where they did the least good. The Patrol had tried helis in the past, but had always come back to ground machines, like the swift turbine still on his tail.

There was occasional traffic on the loop; an unmarked turbine waited to merge in at the next access point.

113

Squawks and phrases rattled over the radiophone. In the rear seat, Rose Ann let out a low, wild cry and wrenched over on her belly, falling on the blankets piled into the well.

Billy couldn't see her down behind the front buckets. His heart began to race. She made another noise, like a cut animal.

"Officers, for Christ's—"

The new turbine slid over behind the Twister and blinked its lights. "We'll ease back, fourteen B. This is Mr. Whitesell who just joined us. He's a traffic counselor with General Ford."

All that Billy saw of Mr. Whitesell was a shoulder-and-head blur inside the turbine now riding directly behind him. What somebody working for the one and only auto manufacturer in the U.S.A. was doing aiding the Patrol, he couldn't fathom; that was just one more confusion among many.

For a minute the radiophone was quiet; shut down at the other end? Then a hollowness indicated the band active again. Mr. Whitesell spoke, sweet and easy as syrup; he talked the way docs talked in telly stories: always sounding one hundred percent right.

"Fourteen B? Bud Whitesell. The Patrolmen explained your situation—"

"They don't really seem to get it. My wife's in bad shape. I need a doc. I got to get off to find one."

"That won't be possible."

"What the shit do you mean, that won't be possible?"

"It isn't possible," Whitesell returned. "We'll have to ask you to return to the highway. We'll do everything we can to see your wife gets assistance, however."

Stunned, disbelieving, Billy digested this latest. He'd expected an arrest. He tried again. "My wife isn't going to get *any* help unless I get off—"

"It's really not possible, fourteen B. You're required to return to the highway. Regulations say—"

"Regulations, what goddam regulations?" Billy shouted. "Are you guys crazy or something? What is all this, regulations? Are you telling me I can't stop?" The whole world had lost its tie rods; the fear melded into rage: "I am gonna stop. Right now!"

"You heard Mr. Whitesell," came the voice of the Patrolman who'd done so much talking before. "Just cooperate and there won't be any problem—"

"There purely hell is a problem! My wife may be *dying!*"

Whitesell said, "But regulations forbid—"

"Regulations, I never heard of such regulations! Who made 'em up? You tell me that!"

"Never mind that. We—"

"Then you tell me what the hell a guy from General Ford is doing, working with the police! Who says I got to listen to you? Who gives you any authority?"

Whitesell sucked in so much air, Billy heard it over the connection: "Fourteen B, if you're going to be difficult, then you'll just delay us. We want to help you find a doctor for your wife—"

"But before that happens, I got to get back up on the highway?"

"Yes, you've got the idea."

Billy told him what to do.

Suddenly Whitesell sounded breathy: "Listen, fellow, we're trying to be of assistance but apparently you won't let us. We don't make these rules. We're just here to enforce—"

"If you can't explain who made up all these god damn rules I never heard of, I don't guess I have to listen." Billy pounded his half-boot down hard on the gas pedal. The Twister roared and accelerated.

Over the intercar wavelength, a mixture of voices—

Whitesell: "He's pulling off! Fourteen B—"

The Patrolman: "Lock on him, Murray, lock on him!"

Suddenly Billy's head damn near went through the windshield. He yelled; the Twister's speed had dropped 15 mph in an instant. A loud buzz seemed to come from under the glittering orange hood. Billy fought waves of dizziness, cricked his neck to ease the sharp pain, booted the gas pedal again.

Nothing happened.

With a curse, he wrenched the steering wheel. He'd show that grease-mouth traffic counselor.

The Twister didn't veer. The power steering plant

115

emitted a sandpapery, overstrained sound. Billy yanked the wheel left, right—

Nothing.

Behind, the Federal turbine swung out to the left. It overtook the traffic counselor's machine, then Billy's. The Patrol car was riding in the lane meant for oncoming traffic; the howler let go again; a light van approaching skidded off onto the service strip to avoid a head-on.

Rose Ann cried out louder than ever. Billy heard a lot of thrashing back there, kept muttering cusswords, as he tried to take control of the Twister again.

He couldn't. It operated at a constant 43 mph, and he couldn't push the speed up, slack it off, or steer. He was losing his goddamn mind.

The Highway Patrol turbine was now directly to the left. The Patrolman driving jockeyed it in close, closer, closer yet. Maniacs! Billy screamed at them.

"You lied to us, Road plate," said the Patrol voice on the radiophone.

Billy shouted, telling them what they could do.

"You are carrying magnetic gear," the voice went on. "Yeh, how do you know?"

"We just locked onto it. We've overridden you. We've got control. Slide over into the right bucket. Your machine will steer itself."

Billy whipped his head left, and goggled.

Instead of opening outward on vertical hinges like conventional machine doors, the right hand door of the turbine slid to the rear, disappearing into the right wall of the back seat. No, not quite disappearing; stars and stripes gleamed faintly through the rear window glass.

The Patrol officer on the right side ditched his hat. His flared lapels snapped in the windstream as he grabbed the upper edge of the open doorframe while the two machines ran twelve inches apart.

A voice on the link, his partner. "You slide over, mister, and damn fast. Officer Stein's taking charge."

Officer Stein didn't fool around waiting for signs of cooperation. He heaved himself up to a half-crouch, hands gripping the upper edge of the doorframe, left boot jammed down on the carpeting in front of his bucket.

116

He kicked out with his right boot, shoved it over and through the open window and into the front seat of the Twister.

Still holding on with both hands, he kicked his left foot over and inside. His heels hit Billy in the face once, twice, three times, till Billy decided not to fight. He hitched across to the right bucket to get out of the way of the big Patrolman who jacknifed his butt in the open window, finally letting go of his handhold on the other car.

A couple of twists, and the officer had his tail firmly in the bucket. He was a big, slab-headed mother with a scraped chin and long yellow hair. He put his left hand on the steering wheel. With his right he pulled his gun.

It was a gun of peculiar design. As far as Billy could tell, it lacked a cylinder. Its barrel was elongated, almost needle-like. Billy knew that Patrol officers carried tranquilizing weapons, but he'd never before seen one pulled.

"You're causing us a hell of a lot of trouble, fourteen B," the officer said. Billy just didn't know what to say, or how to react. So much had happened in so short a time, he couldn't cope. He sat leaning way back against the right door, his brown hair riffled by the stinking night wind.

The Special Officer fiddled with the radiophone as the stars-and-stripes turbine dropped back, slid into line behind the counselor's machine. Officer Stein said, "You can give me control now, Murray."

All at once, the sandpapery grinding in the power steering stopped. A short, ominous *thunk* shook the whole machine. The yellow-haired officer rested that funny gun on his right thigh, its tip angled out ever so slightly, in case it had to be elevated and pointed fast. For his part, Billy was scared.

On the link, the other Federal officer said, "Whitesell's trying to locate the nearest wheeldoc."

That whipsawed Billy into some semblance of a clear head. He fought off his fear to go back to the original problem. "You officers don't believe that my wife is—"

"We believe you. We can't let you take her to a doc down below, that's all."

"I never heard tell of rules like that."

Operating the Twister, the officer gave Billy a most

keen and peculiar stare. Billy couldn't read it. Like curtains, the eyes hid things behind. Stein said, "Maybe not. But there are rules all the same."

Rules. Rules. It sounded vast, powerful; it stirred Billy to a new alarm. *Whose* rules forbade stopping? It was the clan that maintained that a man must continue at no less than 40 mph all his life. How could these people, these men with a huge weight of officialdom riding their shoulders like invisible birds, make up such rules too? Who had the authority? The clans? These men?

Rose Ann cried out. Billy jerked. "Officer—"

"Stein. Stein is my name, and I'd just as leave not have any more trouble. As soon as we find out about the doc, we'll go back upstairs."

Billy rubbed the butt of one palm against the bridge of his nose, trying to drive off sinus pain that had become almost blinding. He rode with his head down, his neck still hurting from the whip, and didn't speak for a minute. He still didn't know what to say; or even where to begin.

He thought briefly of the Firebird. But that big, burning doombird didn't apply here. Nothing applied here; nothing made sense—except the urgency of Rose Ann's cries.

Billy asked if it was all right if he looked at her. Special Officer Stein gave one quick nod. Carefully, Billy hunched around. He clambered up on his knees in the bucket, leaned over. He sucked in a breath.

Rose Ann lay on her right side, sprawled across the blankets in the well. Every time the flash revolved on the Patrol turbine following them, her left cheek glistened with a pink sheen.

Billy rubbed his finger tips in the sweat and felt them. Clammy.

He brushed back a bit of her taffy hair. If she felt it, she didn't indicate. She kept shuddering. He wanted to disturb her, move her, find out how bad the blood had become. He didn't have the nerve. So he rubbed her temple a few more times, full of pain and worry. She started to cry out regularly, softly at first, sort of an "ahhh, ahhh" sound.

"Don't, Rose Ann," he said. "Please don't. We'll get you some help."

118

"Ahhh, ahhh. Ahhh, ahhh."

"Oh, Jesus, Rose Ann honey, stop that, please don't do that."

Special Officer Stein said to the radiophone, impatiently, "Whitesell? Have you got anything yet?"

Several seconds of scratch. Then: "Yes."

"Good. It sounds like his wife's in pretty bad shape."

"Found a wheeldoc about a hundred miles east on the Joshua Tree beltway. He's been re-routed by Western Traffic Central."

"He's coming right through a jam, isn't he?"

"Yes, it may take four or five hours. But he's coming as fast as he can."

Billy looked at Special Officer Stein as the Twister finished maybe its hundredth loop of the loop. "Four or five hours? I can't wait that long. It's already been all day!"

The wet surfaces of Stein's eyes reflected oncoming traffic. The Twister mill bubbled; the superexpressway thundered overhead; the blurred lamps of the meg looked poignantly close.

Stein tried to sound soothing despite the opacity of his expression. "Listen, we're doing our best. Whitesell told you the truth. Maybe we don't like carrying out all these rules, but we have to do it. You've got to go back to the road and that's just the way it is. Traffic Central will do everything it can to get the wheeldoc through as fast as possible."

"*Ahhh, ahhh. Ahhh, ahhh.*"

"It isn't gonna be fast *enough!*"

"Calm down, that doesn't help anybody," Stein said. He addressed the radiophone. "Murray? I'm going up. We'll head for the Joshua Tree beltway and see if we can meet the wheeldoc any sooner."

Billy knelt in the right bucket, his mouth hanging open, his eyes red animal eyes every time the flash went around, *whick.* His fingers flexed.

A murmur over the link indicated that the Patrolman in the stars-and-stripes turbine had heard. Billy wondered why this was happening to him. Christ on the rugged cross —why?

119

"Whitesell?" Stein said. "You want to stick with us?"

"Do you need me?"

"Don't think so."

"Well, all right then. There's a call for me up on the Ventura feeder. It'll take me two or three hours to get there as it is." A pause. "Will you please tell fourteen B—"

"He can hear you," Stein said.

"Fourteen B?"

"What?"

"Nothing personal. I'm only—"

"You mothersticker!" Billy screamed, hitting the radio-phone with his fist. Special Officer Stein whipped up the gun, told him to hold it, but Billy went right on hitting and hollering. "You big-ass mothersticker, don't tell me any more about your goddamn rules! It's the first time I ever heard that a guy couldn't leave the road if he wanted."

Still talking, still ordering Billy to ease off, Special Officer Stein gave him another peculiar stare. Billy didn't pay any attention. He was busy yelling. "I never heard of that before, and instead of explaining why, all you're giving me is a lot of shit about you not making the rules— *whose* rules?" He hit the radiophone again. "*Whose* rules, you tell me!"

"Cutting out," Whitesell said, sounding tired. The band died.

Billy hit the radiophone once more. Then he squatted back with his legs folded underneath him, his shoulders hunched so his head didn't bang the dome of the Twister. The machine picked up speed. Stein held the odd gun upright now, butt braced on his thigh.

A merge-off appeared ahead. The Twister kept accelerating. Stein drove with his left hand; frowned over the touchiness of the power steering. He began to edge the machine to the right.

"You're not really going back up there—" Billy began.

"Ah, come on," the Special Officer said. "Why argue? We already told you—"

Right then, Rose Ann really screamed.

It took about a second for everything in Billy to burn

120

out, fuse together, and he went for the Special Officer's throat with both hands.

He tightened his fingers. The officer yelled, *"Hey!"* Billy tried to kick his knee over to really give it to Stein in the crotch. He screamed words that made no sense. Accelerating, the Twister began to yaw back and forth.

An oncoming stopper machine peeled off, honking wildly, to avoid a crash. *"Hey, goddamit—"* Stein choked, maneuvering the nose of the gun up between Billy's arms. He fired, *chuff*. Something pricked Billy's neck.

Billy fell back, wide-eyed, paralyzed. He cracked his head on the edge of the open right window.

His muscles left him before his mind did. In the back, Rose Ann screamed on a higher note, then a higher one, a higher one still. No doc, no medicine. Billy tried to call her name but his mouth turned to gel. The last thing he saw, Special Officer Stein was fighting the wheel with one hand and trying to look back at Rose Ann, his mouth wide open and—finally—his eyes too.

All the lights of the road came together, then went out.

iii / High Gear

"*Oh God! oh Christ!! oh Jesus!!! it's an awful dream I wake up with sometimes when I'm tooling a soft 90 on the Tulsa Triplepike and it's dark and, sweet Mother of God!!!!, half awake I see it, I see the bonnet all sweet glowing cherryred and aching, aching right toward it and the old pores, Christ on the mount!!!!!, they're bleeding sweat like oil, oh Mercy God I see it in a beautiful vision, the dials revolving, click, in eight places and then I know I'll drive all night I'll drive all day right on the edge, the narrow edge yes I'll drive until I see the Big Fifty yes by the heavenly chrome camshafts of My Lord Jesus's howling chrome superstock I'll see it or I'll die!!!!!*"

—BIG DADDY HARDCHARGER

Baby Rose Ann, what there was of her—a smear, was all Billy could think of afterward, weeping; a smear—died somewhere on the eastbounds of the Joshua Tree beltway. Rose Ann herself survived, although she would never carry another baby as long as she lived. The wheeldoc found it necessary to cut something out.

Billy discovered this when Rose Ann returned to the caravan east of Sacramento four days after Billy's own arrival.

He woke up on a Sunday morning, in his own bed, in his own alcove, in his own quarters in the caravan. He was told by the first person he met outside that the Federal Highway Patrol had returned him, towing the Twister. The Twister had not been confiscated. The Patrol simply delivered Billy and his machine and drove away.

Four days after that, another Patrol turbine returned Rose Ann; Billy had already received a radiophone message from the wheeldoc saying she would survive, but he was keeping her a few days for observation.

When she walked in, she looked extremely pale. Her hair hung uncombed. She wore no makeup. She stared at him with those deep green eyes.

"Hello, Rose Ann."

She said nothing, going in to change her clothes. Billy's head swam; it did that every day, at unpredictable times, a hangover of the knockout dart the officer had shot into his throat. He followed her, feeling the uneasy ride of the living quarters van over an uneven stretch of superhighway.

In the alcove Rose Ann turned her back. She began to loosen the fastenings of her blouse, shuck out of it.

125

Power pylons flashing by outside cast moving swordlike shadows on the synthetic rug. Billy ticked his lips with his index finger, said, "Rose Ann, are you all right?"

No answer.

"Rose Ann, I tried to get you to help, honest to God I did. They wouldn't let me off the highway—I never heard of anything like that before, did you? Rose Ann?"

No answer.

He touched her shoulder from behind. "I been sick worryin' about you—"

No answer, except a slight forward motion of the shoulder; a small move, but definite: separating his hands.

Bottling up his feelings, he tried a tone a little lighter, talking like Uncle Sammy worrying over a mysterious motor problem he couldn't track down:

"Damnedest thing, too. Like—they didn't take the mother away from me. Didn't even lock it up or arrest me for having an illegal machine. And here I've been scared of those crackerheads all my life! They just wouldn't let me off the highway." But that was as long as he could hold back his earnest hurt: "Oh God, you don't know how hard I tried. I begged 'em. Fought 'em, finally. That's when they shot a dart in me." He seized her again. "Rose Ann, I tried. Sweetheart—"

No answer. But she turned her head to look at him. And through him.

Billy made a few more efforts to breach her silence, but Rose Ann simply undressed down to her underthings, crawled under the bedding, pulled it up and over her left side and shut her eyes.

Billy's face was all soft and uncertain. He knew it was no use. He left the quarters as quietly as possible and went to the cafeteria van for a meal.

There, he sat apart, unbothered by companions, or even questions, or even how'd-you-dos. A strange, unfamiliar depression had settled over all the folks as the caravan rolled east to the Sierras. He'd felt it first just after he woke up from the sleepy-dart. It wasn't anger; he saw none of that in their eyes and downturned mouths. It was a silence; an absence of joy. Something had gone wrong.

126

Eudora came by to hand him a message without saying a word. The message contained condolences from the Reverend Cleatus Cloverleaf, and a statement that the preacher had volunteered to travel down from Oregon to handle a proper memorial service for baby Rose Ann. Rose Ann had refused.

Billy stared at the flimsy paper, then crumpled it up and threw it away. He remained at the table a long while, staring at his uneaten grits and seeing nothing. When the cafeteria lights began to blink out, he left.

The door to his quarters was locked, so he moved on.

The October rains slanted down across Oklahoma, all but hiding the glow of the three-county Oklacity meg they were passing, rolling east.

Colonel Tal's bachelor room was located on the right, the southern side of the van. Thus it was shielded from the northerly onslaught of rain. The men, the older and the younger, sat out on the little porch, passing Lightnin' back and forth and brushing away an occasional back-spray of road water churned up by the great slathering tires.

"Can't puzzle it out," Billy began, again.

Tal regarded the storm-hidden, cloud-hidden city across the plain and helped himself to another swig. He did not immediately return the plasto flask.

"I always thought going below 40 mph was tradition," Billy said.

Tal's eyes turned to nuggets. " 'S right."

"But the officers—they were the ones wouldn't let me stop."

"A mystery." Tal murmured. "Can't fathom it out either."

"You ever heard of those traffic counselor fellows?"

"Never did. Never in all my days."

"Funniest thing—" Billy had to keep speaking; when he didn't, he remembered too much of many things. "So damn weird. I mean, here's this fellow, I don't know what his job was, exactly, except to keep me from stopping. He works for General Ford, which is a private outfit. But

127

these two Federals, they were kowtowing to him. Like he was in charge. Weirdest thing."

"I never encountered such a situation," Tal said, his mouth around the bottle. "I never tried stopping."

"Never?"

"Never. You just don't, that's all."

"Yeh, Colonel, but who says?"

"The Spoilers says. The Tollbooths says. The road says."

"I got a different slant on it."

"Well, it's all beyond me," Tal answered in a strangely flat voice. "It's just more of the craziness out there—cities all swole up—stoppers everywhere—bitin' each other like rats in a cage—I'm too old to fret over such." He held out the Lightnin'. "Want some more?"

Billy did; the vans roared, climbing a slight grade.

Billy felt lonely; as lonely as that wide, rainfilled sky above. He began to muse once more. "Just can't puzzle it out, that's all. I believe like I was brought up to believe —don't drop her off below 40 mph; that's the law; that's what a man does. Then here comes the Federals saying the same thing, seems like. Makes you wonder who said it in the first place."

Colonel Tal coughed into his hand. "Wish you wouldn't go over it and over it, boy. Same thing, forty times a night. Not good."

"You don't want to talk about it?"

"What's the point? The Patrol fellas—they got to be crazy."

"How do you figure?"

"It's the road says no stopping, Billy. The road. Why get yourself sick worryin' over one exception? What if it is a mystery? What do you 'spose you can do about it?"

In answer to that, Billy remained silent, for all of a sudden, Colonel Tal didn't seem like so much of a hero, burrowing back into excuses and quarrelsomeness like an old dog disturbed with its favorite old bone. Suddenly Billy didn't think so much of Colonel Tal's twelve grades of education, either. Colonel Tal was trying to make light of what had happened; trying to skip it, as if he were scared of it; scared it'd unsettle things.

Well, it had done that. A mother had been returned unimpounded. Billy had been returned unarrested. That made 'em all nervous. Glum; uncommunicative.

But the real question was—

Why?

Billy had some notions about a way to find out. He wouldn't let Colonel Tal steer him off it, either.

Tal cricked his arm, making a bone pop. He scratched his knee, extended his wrinkly fingers for the Lightnin'. "Where's your wife tonight?"

"Where's she always any more? Out."

"She talkin' to you?"

Now it was Billy's turn to curl up inside, steer off; because this hurt. He said:

"Oh, some."

"Billy?"

"What?"

"Is she steppin' around on you?"

"I dunno. The truth is, I don't much care."

And in fact, Billy didn't. At least not so much that he'd get angry over it.

Oh, it pained him, yes, the whole sad mess, for which he blamed himself most of the time. But he simply couldn't summon any rage whenever Rose Ann slapped his evening meal on the table—place set for one—then primped up and announced she wouldn't be back till late.

Colonel Tal ruminated on Billy's answer a while, peering at the sheeting black rain. Billy had the notion that the older man wanted to talk of Billy's marital problems so they wouldn't veer back to the earlier discussion. Presently Tal let go with an opinion. "A lad with some iron 'tween his legs wouldn't stand for his woman stepping around. I mean, no matter why."

"Jail me," Billy shrugged. "I just can't get very worked up."

"You know, Billy, it ain't no sin for a man and his wife to split up if it comes out that it was a bad job from the beginning. Happens to lots of folks. Maybe it's time you thought some in that direction."

Truly, Billy had. But he always returned to the same

129

starting point: those consuming green eyes; that pretty taffy hair; he loved her.

Christ—sometimes he certainly wished he didn't. But he did, so he wallowed along in a sea of sadness and lethargy, accepting her anger and her bad behavior along with his own guilt. Naturally all this couldn't be told to Colonel Tal. He replied, "Oh, I don't think it's time for that just yet."

"Ummm." Tal drank. Then: "By the way—"

"Yeh?"

"Cousin Hector come in from up Grand Island way last night. He saw a flock of Ramps headin' east."

Billy's palms began to tickle. He reached for the Lightnin', drank.

He might as well have been drinking tapwater. Out behind the rainstorm he saw a flicker of firestreaming wings. Or was that simply in his head? He was chilly; wished he had a sweater.

"Just thought you ought to know," said Colonel Tal.

Late October leafed off the calendar, and there was November with its early sunsets and cold, sleety rains. The Spoiler caravan pushed on east. No one said so much as a word concerning a Christmas-holiday rendezvous with the other clans.

Billy had a lot of trouble sleeping. His mind constantly picked at the puzzle of what had happened with the Federal Highway Patrol officers in California. He daydreamed about it, then had nightmares about it when at last he went to sleep on the sofa, allowing Rose Ann the privacy of the bed, right from the first time she demanded it.

He felt more isolated from the clan than he ever had in his life. One time, over a couple of beers in the vest pocket bar that second cousin Jobe Spoiler had taken over after Nick Spoiler fled, Billy unleashed a few of his theories about how—just maybe—the clan notion that it was unmanly to drop speed below 40 mph was some kind of old fiction; how—just maybe—the people really interested in seeing that it didn't happen were the Patrol officers.

Jobe instantly stopped mopping the bar. "I'm gonna cut

off your poison, cousin Billy." Jobe had sprouted a mustache, and carried himself with an affected dignity now that he'd invested all he had in a business.

"No call to do that," Billy replied. "I'm just thinking out loud."

"You're goin' crazy out loud, is what you're doing."

"But them officers—"

"Billy, you've said a lot, but what you haven't said is the most important thing."

"What's that?"

"The reason! Why anybody'd *want* to keep folks like us from stoppin'."

With a glum shake of his head, Billy admitted, "That I don't know."

" 'Thout that, the rest don't make any sense."

"Guess it doesn't. Still—I can't help thinking—what if we've had it bass ackwards all along? What if we figure we thought up the idea, but we didn't really?"

Jobe slapped his rag down, *plop*. Something uneasy lit his eyes. "I don't want to talk no more about it." He swung away. "I got to check my stock."

Nobody wanted to talk about it. Billy had to find out for himself.

Alone.

The Twister bubbled and rumbled, pelting through the late night rain. A few headlamps came on from the other way. Now and then he passed a commercial vehicle fountaining up water. Otherwise the eight-lane super was light, even for this time of night. It was about four in the morning according to the sleepy announcer who broke into the all-night gospelrock broadcast to give the time, the temperature and the road conditions in the vicinity of the Gateway Arch.

Billy only half heard. His jacket was zippered to the neck. He wore driving gloves against the November chill.

A monster sign loomed up over the lanes.

Chewing his underlip, Billy eased her down out of high. The speedo fell off to 55 mph. He'd passed a stars-and-stripes-decorated turbine about ten miles back. The Patrol machine was heading the other way, west. He hadn't seen a sign of the law since. Raindrops fell through the lightbars of his headlamps. The drops shone like precious stones.

His throat scratched. His heart beat fast. But he had his mind made up. He kept easing off the gas pedal till he had her right about 42 mph.

He slid over to the exit lane that widened out of the right-hand lane all of a sudden. He searched the dark.

Far off eastward there was a suggestion of red heavens behind the rain; that would be the meg along the Mississippi. Nearer, the lights of Springfield marched to the north and south horizons. He hissed down the wet concrete of the exit lane, began to turn, exerting tight control on the touchy power steering.

The down-angling ramp merged into a lower-level freeway, three lanes each way; a local belt running around Springfield, if he read the signs correctly. He was on the local belt in a moment, running half way between the big road above and the rainy streets below.

Down there, isolated streetlamps touched up row on row of stopper bungalows with a cold, bluewhite light. Green signs and exit ramps became more frequent. At 42 mph, he angled over in preparation for turning off.

Throwing off arches of water from under its tires, the stars-and-stripes-decorated turbine roared up out of the dark behind him and pulled around. There were the usual two Special Officers inside. The turbine veered into the exit lane ahead of him.

Billy's whole middle went loose, like knots cut suddenly. He had part of his answer. Or he would in a second, if and when—

Yes.

The tiny red dashlight glowed on, went off. Glowed on, went off.

He dialed the intercar wavelength, picking up, "This is the Highway Patrol, Road plate fourteen B double 2."

"I hear you."

"Where are you going?"

"Into Springfield."

"Afraid you can't do that."

"How come?"

"Never mind, you just follow orders if you want to stay out of trouble." Having pulled about a half mile ahead, the Patrol turbine kicked on its brakes, swung broadside and rocked to a stop, effectively blocking the ramp that led down to Springfield's streets. "Get back in the regular lanes and take the next feeder back to the main highway."

A grin, half smug, half scared, was all Billy gave back to the radiophone. He roared down on the blocking vehicle.

The officer came on again, shouting: "Did you hear the order, fourteen B? Hey, you dumb bastard! Ease off on the speed! Ease off or you'll hit—"

Billy hunched at the wheel. Doing 60 mph, the Twister hurtled at the parked turbine.

The officer on the radiophone yelled blue murder; the turbine switched on its flash and howler. Billy remained on a collision course till the last second, then spun her hard to the left.

He fishtailed on the wet pavement. The back end nearly hit the turbine's left side. He fought the power steering for what seemed like forever, everything blurring and yawing, rainsmeared beyond the windshield glass. He rammed the wheel hard right and poured on gas.

The Twister straightened out in one of the main belt lanes, spurted ahead.

Billy leaned back. That was cutting it fine. But he'd wanted to show those officers his rage. Soon, though, the rage faded away. He was left empty and unsatisfied.

He thought of a number of maneuvers he might make. None seemed worthwhile; an unhappy misery was gnawing all through him.

When he found the feeder leading back to the main, higher westbounds, he took it at 65 mph. Before long, the lamps of Springfield dropped away beneath. He was on the top level, the big road, once more, banging through the night back toward the caravan.

His mind fingered what he'd come out tonight to discover. It was like a paper bag he couldn't open: the outside was recognizable enough; the contents remained hidden.

Not dropping below 40 mph—not stopping—wasn't simply a whim enforced by the Patrol out on the West Coast; no, sir. It was a law they enforced widely. That gave the lie to the idea that it was a road clan tradition.

But that left him hungry: what was the reason? It left him sad and empty: what could be said? Who could be told—that would believe? There were powers loose he didn't comprehend. They terrified him.

Soon something else popped up to grab his attention. A whole string of new, unfamiliar vans rolled behind the Spoiler caravan. Billy looped back, passing them as he barrelled east to bring the Twister home.

A lot of lights burned in the vans, whose configurations Billy suddenly recognized. As he went by the van in the lead, its driver, high in the bubble cab, flashed lights once, twice, three times.

Billy signaled on the radiophone. The rear doors of Sammy's service van folded open. The dragging ramps extended. Billy climbed onto the grabbers.

The sleepy Spoiler boy on all night duty couldn't wait to rush up to the driver's window and exclaim:

"You see them new vans? You know who that is?"

Billy swiped his glove over his upper lip. "Looks like Ramps."

"It is! They merged in from the K.C. freeway 'bout an hour ago. You should hear the talk goin' round. You know who they got with 'em?"

Billy shook his head.

"Big Daddy Hardcharger. Himself!"

Climbing out, Billy stiffened. The bottom was gone from his belly.

"Oh, Jesus, Morris, that couldn't—"

" 'S what I heard. It's what everybody heard. They're lookin for you."

Terrified, Billy took the electric runabout back to his

dwelling van. On the way he made a second loopback, came up a second time past the Ramp vehicles. This time he winced when the lead driver flashed lights. He had an awful bellyache by the time he crept inside his quarters.

A single light burned in the cooking alcove. It showed him Rose Ann sitting up suddenly, the covers clutched to her bosom and a sparkly, happy light in her deep green eyes. For the first time since she'd come back after losing baby Rose Ann, she smiled.

"Hi, Billy. Have you heard? Old Lee Ramp's here. What do you think about that?"

The meeting was called for noon the next day.

Intermediaries haggled over the location, finally agreed on the chapel in the Ramp's general service van. Billy had wanted the confrontation on Spoiler clan territory. But Colonel Tal—already volunteered as Billy's second—said that according to protocol, the Ramps had the choice, since they were the ones whose honor had been affronted; they were the ones doing the calling out. So Billy said okay.

From the moment Billy woke, folks kept stopping by his quarters to repeat the soon-wearisome rumor that Big Daddy Hardcharger, cousin-kin to the Ramps, had come along. Billy didn't want to believe it. He tried to laugh it off. He asked questions, too. Turned out that nobody had actually *seen* the legendary demon driver. So maybe things weren't so bad after all.

Still, Billy felt morbid about the perkiness of all the visitors. They offered plenty of sympathy. But their eyes showed that they had shucked off the moody worry of the last few weeks, and were thrilling to events which, they felt, were bound to come.

Billy wished he had someone close to talk it over with. But when he got up, Rose Ann was already gone. He didn't let himself speculate on where she might be. Or with whom.

A few minutes before twelve, Jobe Spoiler picked Billy and Colonel Tal up in his runabout. He zipped them ahead to a loopback, headed west, looped back again, and over-took the Ramp vans, which generally ran to hysterical fluorescent colors for decoration. Little color besides that showed this November morning. A misty pall pushed down on the superhighway, muffling the sounds of traffic, all but hiding the foul cloud that would have been visible eastward on a clear day over the meg at the Mississippi.

Jobe pulled the runabout behind the general service van, from whose unfolded doors a large piece of white cloth had been hung, signal of safe conduct. Jobe was so nervous, he nearly tipped them over maneuvering onto the grabbers. Colonel Tal cussed him out. Jobe started sweating, mopping his mustache with the back of his hand.

Up inside the van, Billy recognized heavy-bellied, saw-legged Werty, a big grin on his face. Werty flagged them in. He even opened the left door for Jobe.

"Mornin', gents, mornin' to all."

"We don't need that," Tal said. "This ain't no social."

"No," Werty agreed affably, "you're dang right."

"Oh, Jesus in Gethsemane." Billy whipped around at the sound of Jobe's voice. "Oh my God, is that his?"

"Yessir," Werty confirmed. "That's Big Daddy's machine."

Billy swallowed, glimpsing the vehicle parked at the front end of the dank, oily interior. Werty dry-washed his hands like some kind of tourist guide. Jobe, the damn fool, went scuttling up front to have a look.

Tal cast a flinty glance at Billy, whose face was blank. Tal marched off after Jobe. Billy followed.

Never in his born days had he laid eyes on such a mean, chopped-down machine. It had been lowered a good three inches on its chassis, the hood and rear deck reworked into flowing lines—the front of the hood resembled a knife more than anything else. The machine was equipped with the hugest wide boots Billy'd ever seen.

At some time in the past, the basic color of the machine had been white. That background was now all but gone, lacquered over with close-packed, meticulous designs in electric colors: flames, monsters, voluptuous women buck-nude and detailed down to the slenderest hair and the glisten on their wide-open lips. Werty Ramp stumped around front, threw the hood latch, banged her up, beckoned. "Just take a look at this here mill, won't you?"

Billy, Tal, and Jobe peered under like fathers staring

at new babies. Jobe jiggled from foot to foot, gasping, as if he were wetting his pants with fear or excitement or both.

The interior of the engine compartment was immaculate; no drip of grease or drop of oil showed anywhere on the chrome-dipped components. The air intake that stuck up through a cutout in the hood was as big across as a dinner platter, and Billy'd never seen a larger, chunkier i.c. underhood engine. All was bright chrome.

Werty yanked the hood down so fast they had to leap back to keep from having their heads knocked. He said, "There ain't another mill like that in the whole U.S. It can take anything on wheels." A pause for breath; a friendly glance at Billy. "Or anybody."

"But so far," Tal countered, "it could be any driver's machine."

"Oh, yeh? Poke your head inside. Take a look at the speedo."

One by one, they did. Billy went last. He saw a speedo built into a specially widened recess in the dash. The speedo was complete to eight places, not counting tenth-of-miles. The numerals read 34,283,911.

"Big Daddy's got a good leg up on the Big Fifty, don't he?" Werty remarked. "He wouldn't of quit driving top speed except this is family business. He come all the way from Wyoming. You can drive plenty fast in Wyoming and Montana, Big Daddy says. Up to a hundred-ten, a hundred-twenty, and nobody gives a hoot."

All this Billy only half heard; he was still inspecting the interior of the machine. It was stripped to the essentials: wheel; floorshift; foot controls; radiophone; a single bucket with no retaining straps; rollbars exposed under the dome. By contrast to the engine compartment, the interior was a living mess: full of girly and motor magazines; rotting fruit peels; half eaten burgers still in their waxine envelopes; a closely tooled calf boot with an inch sole and a three inch heel; dirty underwear; a pair of girl's red panties; a discarded condom. The whole conglomeration smelled foul.

"They're waitin' for you up in the chapel," Werty announced. The Spoilers started to the stair leading to the

137

catwalk. Werty restrained Jobe by the arm. "Just two. that's the rules."

With an uneasy glance, Jobe let the others proceed.

Billy took the clanging stairs first, trying to step smartly in order to hide the mounting fear inside him. A vision of those eight places burned across his inner eye. Evidently the same subject concerned Colonel Tal; Billy grew aware of the older man's voice, more graveled than usual:

"—first time I heard of Big Daddy, I didn't believe there was any such person. But I was curious about those stories. You know, how he's goin' to see the Big Fifty 'fore they haul him dead from under the wheel. I did some calculating."

Billy watched the rectangle of the door coming up at the end of the catwalk. The Ramps didn't favor much interior light; the corridors beyond the door had a gray quality.

"Yeh? Did you?"

"Calculated that if a youngster was born movin'—in the clans, y'know—and didn't die till he was seventy or thereabouts, and if the machines he was riding in or driving averaged right about eighty, he could travel—lemme see, I memorized it once—'round forty-eight million, nine hundred twenty thousand and some-odd miles. 'Course now, when you add in the extras—you know; like the just plain illegal speeds that this Big Daddy's supposed to drive at, averagin' ninety or a hundred most of the time—why, he could be plenty younger than seventy when he sees those numerals roll around for fifty million miles. But I never truly believed that any such person—"

Billy raked the air with his hand as they studied the corridor from the doorway. Colonel Tal apologized.

Billy stared at him. The old man—the old hard charger, himself—was petrified.

Billy's spirit's sank another notch.

Fragmented light gleamed way down on their left, beyond double doors standing open at the corridor's end. Billy walked that way, Tal following. Doors along the corridor identified the various shops, services:

Arthur Ramp
Doctor of Chiropractic

All the doors were shut. Several fixtures were out, hadn't been repaired, accounting for the bad lighting. Billy noticed cracks and gaps in the floor tiles, paper wrappers and dirt along the plasto baseboards.

The split-up light dappled the half dozen rows of pews inside the little chapel. The light fell through an imitation stained glass of the Lord Jesus with His lambs, the window itself set high in the forward end of the chapel; the van's front end, above the driver's bubble. Up in the front pew, two men waited.

One man was seated. One stood. The seated one rose up; Billy recognized the slit that served for a left eye.

Lee held his gloved left hand close to his left ribs. His whole body cocked to the left because of the shortening on that side. Patches of dull green and blue and red light from the window dappled the scar tissue on the left side of his face, creating a look of spoiled meat.

But the man to whom Billy's eyes were riveted was the standing one; the smaller.

His height was no more than five four or five. But he had a powerful trunk and shoulders. His legs were bowed. His tooled boots had the same thick soles and elevating heels Billy had noticed in the mother downstairs. His blues, in contrast to Lee's clean ones, had so many spots of so many assorted shapes, sizes, and colors that Billy couldn't count them all. The man's hair was long, flowing, uncut. It tangled down over his ears to merge with a beard that hung to the midpoint of his chest. His three-inch belt was studded with chromed pyramids. The contour of the man's lips indicated no teeth. He might have been forty. He had eyes like a hound's, and wore shiny gloves which he kept flexing.

"Morning," said Lee Ramp.

"Morning," Colonel Tal answered for them.

"Big Daddy, this yere's Talmadge Spoiler. You his second?"

Tal nodded.

139

" 'Side him is Billy Spoiler. Meet my cousin, Big Daddy Hardcharger."

Tal never offered his hand, nor made the slightest move to a polite hello. Billy gave the old man credit: if he was still rattling inside, he was managing to cover it pretty well now. Tal did say, "This is kind of like meeting a ghost."

"Well," said Big Daddy, "I goddam sure ain't a ghost, and let's not make a big jaw out of this, because I've got drivin' to do. Lee here got in touch. Since it's family, I hadda come. Now—" The hound's eyes fixed on Billy. "You the one's gonna settle with me?"

"Guess so," Billy answered.

"No guess about it," said Lee.

Tal's eyes strayed up to the bland, whitemilk-glass face of Jesus over the pulpit. "I sort of thought you might have done your own settlin', Lee."

Lee's voice grew sharply whiny. "Don't you hand me any snotmouth talk like that." He wiggled his tiny, gloved left hand. "You know what this cocker did to me, pulling dirt on me—"

"Let's be straight," Billy broke in. "You did it first."

"Makes no goddam difference who did it first," Big Daddy interrupted him, starting to stump up and down in the tiled aisle between front pew and raised pulpit. "Lee asked me to help out, and nobody's going to waste my time bullshitting about whether he should of or shouldn't of." The hairy head swung. "I'm here. I don't come no-place 'less I feel my kin need me. So that settles that."

Lee leaned his right knee on the front pew. His shorter left leg stayed straight as a rod at his side. His eyes grew all the meaner. "Truth is, I can just about drive like I used to. It's been a long, slow job, learning it all over again." *Slap* went the right hand, over the hip to the left leg and the silver brace hidden under the clean blues.

"Things like reaching for the brake with a left kicker that isn't as long as it used to be."

"As a matter of fack," said Big Daddy, "when Lee here first got me on the phone, sort of to discuss it, he was foolin' with the idea of calling you out himself. He wanted to know what I thought 'bout that idea. I told him what

140

I thought, which is, family's family, even though the Ramps an' me don't see eye to eye on powerplants. I said to him, Lee, long as you want something done, something that needs doin' so there won't be no more shit on the family's face, why, it's just sense to pick the best man to go out and do it." Big Daddy hooked his gloved thumbs in his pyramid-studded belt and rocked back on his heels.

Billy had a momentary impulse toward laughter. But he braked right away. Big Daddy wasn't funny.

"Now," said Big Daddy, "if we don't have to futz away no more time explainin' things to you two, let's get down to details."

Billy edged his hand over to the nearest pew for support. He hoped no one saw. He said, "Okay, Lee, I know what you want. A speed and distance run to settle—"

Big Daddy hawked and spat on the tiles. "Shit."

"You got something else in your mind?" Colonel Tal asked.

Lee leaned still farther forward over the back of the pew. "Are you serious? After all we've swallowed from you Spoilers? You need some fresh oil if you think I'll tally up with just speed and distance like the last time."

"We're gonna have oursels a run. I mean a *run*," Big Daddy said. He marched up to Billy, who caught a whiff of him, grease and sourness and garlic too. "Spoiler boy, I'm callin' you for the flat out. You and me's gonna have a death drive, nothin' less."

Suddenly he grinned, showing his gums.

Billy, taller, still went screaming yellow in his insides for one second. Big Daddy waved a glove under his snoot.

"And guess who's gonna come back? I just got to come back, because I can drive the ass off anybody born. Besides"—the hound eyes glowed madly—"I already seen the Firebird."

Billy expected Jesus to crack and splinter in His windowframe; he expected the van to wreck and the earth to shake. But nothing happened.

An easy grin swiped across Lee's mouth. "He did, too. That's a fact."

"A man sees the Firebird before he dies," Tal said.

"Can't help what you think," Big Daddy shrugged.

Walking up in the direction of the pulpit, he spun on his platformed heel. "I seen it, man. Three years ago, when some cocker challenged me up on the Trans-Oregon. Right purty the bird was, too. The cocker forced me over, near spun me out. I thought I was gone, and there she was—the bird an' the gash riding him with the fire 'tween her purty legs. The gash was squeezin' her own big titties and lookin' like she was ready to come—I saw it all in a flash. Then I brought the ole mother back out of the slide and the bird went away, and I caught up with that cocker and crash-assed him and I killed him dead." Big Daddy twisted the end of his beard. "Just like I'm gonna kill you."

Colonel Tal cast his eye up at Jesus and shivered at the blasphemy in a sanctified place. Lee began:

"Tal and me will work out the details."

"Make sure we wait a while," Big Daddy advised him. "I'll stay in my mother and keep rollin' while we wait a few days. That builds up a nice crowd. We want to be sure to have plenty on hand. This is a big thing. I mean, I wheeled her all the way down from Wyoming, right?"

He marched to Lee, waving his glove, lecturing, almost:

"Also, part of the terms is, we wait till we get a real nasty streak o'weather. Shouldn't have to wait long, this time of year. Bad weather lends more sport," he grinned over his shoulder. "Let's work out the roadway real good, too. Some of these pissy-ass supers ain't worth nothing. Flat. Straight. Real easy banks and grades. We want somethin' tough."

Colonel Tal swiped his hand in front of his face once, impatiently. Lee cocked a brow. "Yeh?"

"You're making a hell of a lot of conditions we got to agree to if—"

"That's right," Big Daddy nodded briskly, "you got to agree, you Spoilers. Unless, o'course, you want to say no, and come out laundered yella the rest of your lives. That's why we decided to talk, don't y' see? We got nothin' to lose." He grinned. "You fellers decide."

The little trap went *ping*, shut tight. For a minute Billy wanted to scream, because this choice was no choice: yellow out, or run against Big Daddy.

Billy didn't honestly know whether he believed all Big

142

Daddy's bragging. Had he seen the Firebird? Really, truly seen it?

No, that made no sense at all.

And yet, watching the cocky little rooster, Billy saw a lot more than swagger.

Maybe what he saw existed only in his mind's eye. Either way, an empty futility overcame him. He rested in the trap.

"You want to yellow out," Lee shrugged, "feel free."

"But if you decide to run," Big Daddy emphasized, "we run in Big Daddy's kind of weather, on Big Daddy's kind of super—or we don't run."

"Nobody'd blame us for turning down a rotten deal like this," Tal said.

"Oh, wouldn't they?" said Lee, twitching his tiny, ruined hand.

Billy let out a long, listless sigh. His sinuses hurt. He said, "Sure they would, Colonel. You know they would."

"He did the dirt first!" Tal exclaimed.

"And he"—Big Daddy's gauntlet pointed—"did the cripplin'. Come on, boys. How much longer do I have to stand here and bullshit? I got the Big Fifty to think about, y'know." He began to punch his right gloved fist into his left gloved palm and bounce up and down on his elevated boots. "Come on, now, come on."

Lee Ramp asked, "Is it yes or no?"

Blind with sweat, Billy waved, "Oh, you know—yes."

"Right fine!" Big Daddy exclaimed, stumping up the aisle. "You seconds work out all the details, I got me drivin' to do."

Without even thinking, Billy hauled back out of the little man's way. Tal whitened at the mouth. Lee snickered.

Big Daddy didn't miss that, either. He chopped to a halt, rocking. His head barely reached to Billy's chin. But that didn't stop Big Daddy from raising his left hand and laying it on Billy's shoulder as he remarked, "Anyway, boy, you'll get a look at the Firebird this way. Real purty. You'll see."

And slapping his greasy thigh he stumped on out of the chapel.

After much haggling—for which Billy didn't have to be present, thank God—Colonel Tal Spoiler and Lee Ramp worked out the details of the route; largely to the latter's satisfaction.

The course agreed on was a stretch of superway running from mid-Kentucky down to the southern border of Tennessee; a stretch that, upon occasion, turned twisty through the mountains from Corbin and Jellico on southward. Billy began studying the run route as soon as he learned of it; maps were easy to come by of a sudden, from vendors who buzzed from van to van hawking cheap field-glasses and the maps with the route color-marked.

And the vans gathered: Tollbooths; Johnsons; Cloverleafs. From as far away as Vermont and Arizona. They rolled along side by side, three lanes wide, down through the Illinois flatlands in the November rain; over the lower side of Indiana; on across the Ohio, muddy and swollen with melted sleet; thence into hilly gray Kentucky. The caravan grew so large that arrangements had to be made for special clearance from the Federal Highway Patrol, as if the clans were holding holiday early.

No mention was made to the Patrol about the death drive, of course. Not a whisper to the outside, even though observant Federal officers might have noted an unusual influx of vans from both north and south.

Two weeks in November passed; fourteen days of clear, sharp, mid-thirties weather. Then, on Thursday prior to Thanksgiving, the national meteorological forecasts began to grim up suitably. Colonel Tal brought word that Saturday night would likely be it.

Ah, the rippling excitement in the caravans; what a stroke of lucky timing! A Saturday night was the best hurrahing night of the whole long week.

According to the forecast, storms of freezing rain were moving in rapidly with a front that was dropping down across Nebraska and Missouri. When Billy took the news in Jobe Spoiler's bar, he merely nodded and went on pouring down Lightnin'. He seemed oblivious to the shiny, jolly eyes and the backslaps of all those who clamored around him, wishing him well.

Friday night, Rose Ann spread the supper table with the first truly big, cooked meal Billy'd seen in quite a few weeks. She busied and fussed over each dish: synthetic roast; mash potatoes; quikbake cornbread; gravy; even a savory apple pie thawing and bubbling in the oven while the rest went on the table. It all smelled fine, heavy, nourishing. But the second Billy sat down, he lost his appetite.

Not that some sickness had overcome him. In fact, he'd hardly thought about the drive all day. He'd been over to Uncle Sammy's van, putting a fine tune on the Twister, and generally checking things out. Several times, without any warning, he found himself deviling with the problem of why he couldn't stop. Now, as he hitched up his chair and realized he should make some comment about the meal, the puzzle came rushing back and killed his appetite.

Rose Ann sat down opposite him. She was fixed up; painted; combed. She looked cheerful. Usually she didn't hum or fix up until later in the evening, when she was preparing to step out alone. Billy tried to focus on this instead of on the puzzle. Outside, he heard the first sleet.

Rose Ann forked some mash potatoes with great concentration. She looked at them, not at her husband. "Billy?"

"Yeh?"

"You scared?"

"Truth is—I'm not."

That disturbed her. "Why to mercy not?"

He looked at her, long and slow, and almost arrived at the point of telling her, in total detail, his puzzlements and concerns. Then a weariness in him just gave up on that. He put her off with, "Oh, I don't know, Rose Ann. Guess this cold weather's wore me out."

"That Big Daddy, he's an awful man. I saw him yesterday. Seems to me you ought to be worrying how to beat him." She'd put down the mash potatoes, and was watching him closely; he recalled the same gleam in her eyes before he and Lee Ramp raced for her.

Suddenly she reached across to squeeze his hand. "Oh Billy, maybe we can make things right again. I mean, you're going to run for me tomorrow night, aren't you?"

In a calm voice he answered, "Rose Ann, I'm going to run against Big Daddy because I have to. With a call-out like his, a man's got no choice. It's either run or yellow out."

Whip, she took her hand away. "Oh, so you're not running for me?"

His mouth quirked. He raked his hair with his right hand, put some effort into thinking how to make the words come out correctly. "Sure, it's *because* of you, but—"

Silence. He shook his head, then dove into potatoes and gravy.

"But what? Billy Spoiler, you answer me. But what?"

Trying not to sound so harsh as to hurt her, he let it come: "Rose Ann, nothing I do will fix it up between us."

"You sound like you don't even care."

"What are you trying to do, Rose Ann, rile me again?"

"Trying to get you to act like something besides an old stone statue."

Bleak in the eyes, he said, "Look, Rose Ann. I'm sorry for what happened about the baby. Sorrier than you'll ever know. But I know it was a mistake."

"The baby?"

He said to his food, "Us."

"In other words, Mr. Billy Spoiler, you just don't give a damn about me?"

"I love you, Rose Ann. I love you a lot, I really do. I always will. But even so"—he dropped his fork, *clack,* forcing himself to look again—"I still got the feeling we're all wrong, and probably were from the start. I don't know if that makes any sense to you, but it's the way I feel."

Rose Ann seemed to shrink a little, retreat back into her chair, blinking and dabbing at her lipstick with her throwaway napkin. Another silence began, and stretched out, and stretched out, while Billy wondered how he could love her and feel so little.

Probably because hopelessness had finally set in; the kind of hopelessness that had dogged and deviled him before their marriage. Way back then, he'd known she wasn't built for settling. Trying to soften that message backfired on him all of a sudden:

146

"You don't care what I'm doing nights, is that what you mean, Billy?"

"I got a fair idea of what you're doing, Rose Ann."

"It doesn't burn you up?"

The food went bad in his mouth. "No, Rose Ann, I'm sorry—not much."

He hoped she'd drop the subject. The corners of her mouth tightened out white and she leaned into the table, forearms on the throwaway tablecloth. "I could tell you about some of the boys I been seeing, Mister Statue. Think that'd thaw you out?"

"Go ahead if you want, I don't care." His mind wandered off to questions about the Federal Highway Patrol; why they wouldn't permit him to stop.

"Some of 'em you know real well. Some of 'em are your own good friends, how does *that* strike you?"

"Well," he said, "after Nick, you don't expect me to be surprised, do you?"

"Then there's old Lee—"

"Aw come on, Rose Ann, don't push it any more."

She refused the plea, her cheeks already colored up. "Old Lee's been sticking pretty close to our vans, did you notice that?"

"Rose Ann, he's a poor cripple. No better than half a—"

"Don't you fool yourself, Billy Spoiler," she broke in with a sweet smile. "Old Lee Ramp's still a pistol, a regular fireball, I give you my personal word. Want to know something else?" She rose, circled the table, almost a stalking figure, her body bowed forward in tension. "I'm half way thinking about being Lee's girl again, wedding papers or no wedding papers. I don't give a damn about what the old ladies'll say, either. A woman needs certain things and oh boy, can old Lee deliver, what do you think about that?"

He didn't say anything.

"Well, what'd you say if I told you that I was going off with Lee first chance I get? Even crippled, he's better than you are!"

Billy simply lifted his head and stared. "Is that right?"

"You bet it's right!" She leaned in really close, mouth

all twisted. "Like to hear some of the juicy details? Like me to tell you exactly how old Lee's better'n you?"

He pushed his plate aside, skidded his chair back, got up and walked away. "No, thanks. I wouldn't."

He heard her coming, didn't turn in time, absorbed the sudden flurry of her fists on his back for a moment. Then he dodged aside, grabbing hold of her wrists and holding her at arm's length, not to hurt, only to restrain.

Rose Ann's cheeks ran with tears. "What's the *matter* with you, Billy? What's inside you, motor parts?"

"Let's drop it, okay? I got other things to think about."

She kept crying, loudly, but he felt he could release her. She didn't strike again.

He opened the draperies, slid the window aside, went to the porch and stood leaning into the bitter night sleet. In the distance to the north he saw the misty lights of the Kentucky and Ohio megs sprawled along the river. The wind picked up Rose Ann's voice and gave it a higher pitch:

"You tell me what's so damn important! You just tell me!"

He turned with his back to the storm, and because there was no point in hauling out all his concerns over the stopping problem, he made up some things that were partly true. "Oh, like whether I got the Twister tuned up just right. How bad traction's going to be tomorrow night. Things like that."

"You know what's killed us, Billy? Do you know?"

"No, Rose Ann, but let's not—"

"Those damn machines. Those goddamn machines. You care about them more than you care about another single living human person. You're just like all the rest. You love those goddamn pieces of junk more than you could ever love anybody. My papa, Lee—you're all alike —a woman's just second, always second."

She was really crying now, wailing through hands that covered her eyes. Suddenly she whipped her hands down and cried, "That's what ruined us, Billy, you're just like all of them; you'd rather stick it in a machine if you could than treat a woman proper!"

The wind broke the last words, giving them a gusty

148

sound. Something cool, final and strange fell over Billy, like a revelation from heaven. "Rose Ann, is that why you worry so much about making men pay heed to you?"

"Isn't it true?"

He thought a minute. He thought of the superhighway under him, unrolling in the dark, running on south, running on north, running on eastward and running on west. His whole life was bound up and summed up in it and by it; his only mastery of it came from the gaudy orange machine parked in Uncle Sammy's van.

He'd never thought about it this way; never thought about loving the machine that was part of, extension of, the endless road. But maybe he did love it. Maybe they all loved it, with a wordless love. He said, "I guess you could be right."

"We never had a chance from the start, Billy. No woman who wants a man to give a damn about her ever has a chance."

"Guess I haven't been showing I care much tonight, either, huh? Guess that's why the hate's so bad on your face?"

Abruptly, Rose Ann spun and sped for the bed alcove. She began to change her blouse, then fixed her face with furious swiftness.

Billy puzzled and worried over the new idea. It had implications much too deep for him. But he did feel that, at last, he maybe understood part of the reason they'd made such a mess.

Maybe she'd hoped she'd turn out the stronger; hoped she could make him forget the road, the machine. She'd failed. Maybe that's why she stepped around. Maybe deep down, she was weary and sick. Maybe at her young age she already knew she'd lost the whole battle.

A tenderness so deep it nearly made him cry rose up through him and he started to her, "Oh, Rose Ann, honey—"

She ran for the door. Ran, crying—or laughing?

"Old Lee, he'll keep me company. I just hope one thing. I just hope tomorrow night you get killed!"

Then she was gone. Billy stood awkwardly, his hands reaching out to the air.

Half a dozen of his best kin, including Uncle Sammy and second cousin Jobe, showed up at eight Saturday night to help him prepare.

Billy paced back and forth beside the Twister while Uncle Sammy topped her off with the highest octane racing fuel available. Billy would have to re-fuel somewhere below the Kentucky-Tennessee border—if the race lasted that long.

The rear doors of the service van already stood open. The dragging ramps had been lowered, even though Billy wasn't due at the start line—the Berea, Kentucky, off ramps—for another half hour.

Despite being zippered up tight in his best driving jac, Billy felt cold. Probably because it was damn cold outside; a mixture of rain and snow whipped into the service van. Scanning out the rear doors and across to the northbound highway, Billy could barely make out the tail-lamps of other vehicles. All the men seemed especially fidgety.

"What are you all hopping around for?" Billy asked finally.

Uncle Sammy forced a smile. "Oh, nothing, Billy. It's just a big night, that's all."

"Damn right it is," chimed in one of the others. "You're going to take him."

"Sure," Billy said. "Did Tal leave already?"

"Yessir." Jobe went through a lot of waste motion, polishing and polishing the driver's side panels till the orange surface shone. "The Ramp's pace machine come for him about fifteen minutes ago. They headed up the line to the start."

"Lee driving pace?"

"Yes, he is," Uncle Sammy confirmed.

"How's traction?" Billy wanted to know.

"Bad," another cousin advised him. Billy looked away and so did the cousin; both were bothered, in different ways, by the man's ill-concealed excitement. Billy swung on the group suddenly.

"I wish you'd all let loose with what's bothering you. You might as well. It's all over your faces."

Uncle Sammy waved, too fast. "Listen, Billy, truly, it's nothing."

"Oh, why don't you go ahead and tell him?" Jobe said.

"Go ahead," Billy said. Then, pushing a grin, "Come on, Sammy."

Uncle Sammy looked positively sheepish. "Billy, don't take this wrong."

"I won't, don't worry. Come on, what is it?"

"Well, it's just that the boys and I would purely love to see the start of the run."

Relieved, Billy guffawed. "Is that all! Take off!"

"We don't want to leave you here all by yoursel—"

"Don't know why not. I can get started all right. All I got to do is turn her over and throw her in reverse and back her to the ramps and let the grabbers do the rest. Listen, you boys wind up your machines and go. The driver can pull up the ramps and shut the doors by automatic. Who's driving tonight, anyway?"

"Ferd Spoiler," Jobe volunteered. "There's just him and a few kids and womenfolk left aboard." Then, with another half-shamed grin: "We all drew straws to see who'd stay. Ferd lost."

Billy put on another big grin. "Ferd always was a loser." Then he started shoving and jostling them good-naturedly. "Come on, now—Sammy, Jobe, Phil—you all go get your machines and head out. Just shut down the inside lights before you go, I don't need those. I'll see you up the line."

Jobe started off. But Uncle Sammy, carrying the authority of the group, hovered, undecided. Billy screwed up his face with false fierceness. "Sammy? What are you waiting for? Look, I'd helluva lot rather have you down by Corbin cheering for me when I bust Big Daddy's bumpers. That's going to be a sight worth watching. I aim to tell my grandchil—" He changed thought without pause. "You all go on."

"Sure you don't mind, Billy?"

"Naw, I want you to go. You're my clan. You got to be there to see it."

Uncle Sammy stepped in close. "Billy—you are gonna take him?"

"Of course I'm gonna take him."

With much whooping, hollering and good wishes, they began shutting down lights in the interior of the service level. Jobe revved up Phil's family wagon in the lext lane over.

All the Spoilers piled in, waving and goodbying and give-him-helling, and Billy threw the switch allowing them to back over into the single set of floor channels that led to the drags. They backed down, eased off, then sped ahead out of sight after flashing lights twice to wish him well.

The inside of the service van was black now. But enough light drifted in from outside so that Billy had no trouble finding his way to the Twister and settling in the bucket.

He twiddled his thumbs.

Ran a mental check of everything he'd done to put the Twister in the finest shape ever. Scratched an itch on the underside of his chin; it wouldn't stop itching.

Plucked the jac where it bound his sweating armpits. Listened to the *whoosh-ROAR, whoosh-ROAR* of clan vans rolling past every minute or so—God amighty, would there be a crowd watching tonight!

A couple of minutes before his time to depart, he was seized by an overwhelming urge to forget the whole thing.

He bent over the wheel a while. Finally he got hold of himself. He wiped his cheek, straightened up and hit the key.

The i.c. mill started with a blast of sound. Billy's breathing picked up, low and reedy over his teeth. *All right, now, hold on,* he thought, for he was wild with nerves already. He kicked the Twister into reverse too fast, starting with a jerk that was plain bad driving.

Over the thunder of the mill, he thought he heard somebody call his name. He kept backing, convinced that he was losing his grip. He'd better tighten down or he wouldn't be worth a hoot against Big Daddy.

Steering, heading backwards to the dragging ramps, he found the power steering unusually tight, unresponsive. He swung the wheel over too far. His right rear tire hit the channel rim too fast, bounced up—a heavy thumping shudder went through the Twister's back end—and he had

152

only seconds to correct, shove the wheel hard left so that the rear tires banged back down into the channel.

He straightened the machine with a wild twist of the wheel and went barrelling onto the drag ramps so fast that the Twister whanged its underbelly.

All of a sudden his hood was angled at the sky. The grabbers whined and grated—iced up already!

The Twister slid down to the highway. The rear wheels hit the pavement too fast. The shock lifted the rear end way up and made the Twister groan.

The instant the front tires hit the pavement, the machine began to slip to the right. Damn ice! He got control through the steering, but it was really acting up: slow; thick; tighter than ever. He broke out in cold sweats as he jockeyed the machine back to the left, clear at last of the ramps than began retracting into the blacked-out lower level of the van.

The road here was six lanes each way. Every lane was slicked by snow that wasn't altogether snow, nor completely rain. Billy eased on the gas, shifted up, finally felt the mother steady throughout. He began to accelerate past the van. As he went by the front end, poor old Ferd Spoiler hit the lights, three blinks—good wishes; farewell.

He'd gone no more than two miles when the traffic began to thicken up considerably. He passed eight vans with orange roofs—Johnsons—on his left. They flashed lights; nobody loved Ramps and Hardchargers. Soon Billy had no more than two lanes in which to drive. The two on his right and the two on his left were full of vans and individual clan machines. Everybody was really looking forward to a show, it seemed, and anxious to tag along despite the weather being so miserable.

An overhead sign:

BEREA
USE NEXT FOUR EXITS

Murky lights gleamed both east and west of the elevated super as Billy turned on the speed and peered forward intently, watching for signs of the pace machines.

153

Pretty soon he picked up the red gleams of Colonel Tal's purple-flake mother. He steadied down to a safe distance behind the Colonel. The radiophone blinked.

"Billy?"

"Right here, Colonel Tal."

"How you feel, son?"

"Okay, Colonel Tal."

"She's a regular slippery bitch under the tires."

"Yessir, I got the feel already."

"They're 'bout a mile ahead. Shall we catch them now?"

"Yes, Colonel Tal, let's catch them."

"Billy—you're a fine lad. I'd be proud to have you for a blood-son of my own. I want you to know that."

Touched, Billy stammered, "Y-yes, sir, thanks a lot."

"Just one more thing, Billy."

"Yes, sir, what's that?"

"You know the stakes tonight."

"Oh, yes, sir, I know."

"I prayed a special prayer to God today, Billy, and you know I'm not a praying man. I want you to come out right. You hold onto that wheel and you drive like you've never driven in all your born days. You kill that cocksucker."

Billy swallowed. "Yes, sir, Colonel Tal. What do you say we go?"

Accelerating, they charged right up the left of the two open lanes, Tal beginning to flash his lights, Billy riding right on his tail.

Truth to tell, he didn't feel all that frightened. Every ounce of his attention was concentrated on the trickiness of the road. He hadn't hit a dry, safe patch yet; and he didn't care for the way the power steering behaved, so glue-slow, with a peculiar little grind in it whenever he had to touch up his forward course. The mixture of snow and rain flashed at his windshield like illuminated needles. It gave him a slight headache—oh yes, there was plenty enough to worry about. He hardly felt anything when he pulled up alongside Big Daddy Hardcharger's garishly decorated mother.

Some sort of phosphor paint had been employed on the

154

finish; all the monsters, flames, and nude women gave off an unusual degree of reflected light. Billy couldn't make out much of Daddy—a couple of black patches for eyes; a smear for beard behind sleet-streaked glass. Big Daddy lifted his right glove close to the glass and gave him the finger; Billy made that out, all right.

Then, in a lightburst, the sparkly overhead arch of another great sign was on him:

LAST BEREA EXIT 1 MILE

He tightened down on the wheel.

Lee Ramp's low, nasty turbine and Tal's purple-flake mother ran hub to hub. Both drivers lay on their horns to clear adjoining lanes. A huge Tollbooth hauler cut back its speed. Another van did likewise over on Lee's right. As the machines flashed by the great green-shining Berea exit board, Tal veered away left, Lee Ramp veered away right, leaving Billy and Big Daddy Hardcharger alone in the center two lanes, running.

Billy's speedo showed an even 70 mph.

Big Daddy wasted no time. He whipped over and socked Billy hub-to-hub.

The shuddering impact nearly sent the Twister into a skid. Billy fought to right himself, twisting the wheel one way, another, cursing the unexplained unresponsiveness of the power steering plant. Flames and monsters loomed up on his right—*wham,* another hit, harder than the first.

But Billy had better control now. He eased out of the bang with less trouble, wrenched the wheel to crash the Twister into Big Daddy's left front wheelwell.

Only Big Daddy's mother wasn't there. All at once Billy was arrowing toward the right lanes with nothing in front of him except dark and slush.

Lights glared in his rearvision; ah, that explained it. The tricky bastard'd braked off fast, and was behind him.

Traveling straight, Big Daddy rammed up and hit the

tail end of the Twister as it shot across the highway at an angle.

The front end of the orange mother began to come around. Big Daddy braked, spinning and sliding himself. But he got clear of Billy, who was slowly skating into a circle, out of control.

The rear boots kept sliding left, left. But even as Billy went into the spin, he still carried some forward motion. In a second, he could look for a shattering crash through the guardrails, and off, dropping through the dark.

He rode the wheel mercilessly, maneuvering so fast that he wasn't even conscious of it. Somehow he brought her out—only he was heading the wrong way—roaring at 50 mph into the monster headlamps of a family van coming at him from half a mile back.

Throat full of a lump, Billy cut right, starting into a U. Would he clear the oncoming van in time? His turning radius was not small. Vans were howling up in the far left lanes, too; with sliding adding to his momentum, he just might blast into one of them before he finished the semicircle.

Through his closed windows Billy heard the blare of horns; saw the amber emergencies begin to blink on vans in right and left lanes. He kept skidding, turning. Almost around now. Almost—but the big Johnson van in the left lane didn't seem to be braking in time. Billy was going to skate into it.

The van driver really laid on the brakes. Billy slid into the extreme left lane, sideglanced the median rail, fought the shudder till the Twister headed out straight.

Driving under some measure of control again, he let the trembling work out of his shoulders and upper arms through his hands. He changed lanes, to the right, changed lanes again, till he was in the lane immediately to the left of Big Daddy's mother. Then he began to move up fast. This time, he'd knock that cocker right in the head.

He hunched forward, concentrating. He pushed up into the 80 mph range, gaining on Big Daddy, gaining.

Suddenly, Big Daddy's mother seemed to leap forward. Slush spurted from under its rear tires; some splattered over on Billy's windshield. Big Daddy's machine grew

156

smaller in seconds. By the time Billy reacted, Big Daddy was a good mile, mile and a half ahead, traveling—how fast? 100 mph? 110 mph? On *this* kind of road?

"Damn maniac," Billy said. "Damn crazy loony maniac."

Smears of slush whipped off his windshield. He could just fancy Big Daddy up there laughing at him; snickering to beat hell because he'd made a fool of Billy: waited for Billy to catch up, then ran away, showing him his tail. Now Big Daddy was really moving, over 100 mph for certain.

Billy edged up into the 90 mph range. The Twister grew wobbly, riding the raw edge of out-of-control. A yeasty lump formed in Billy's throat again. Big Daddy was daring him, challenging him; Billy'd look yellow if he failed to match the speed.

His eyes flicked over to the northbounds. Jesus nailed up bleeding! He'd never seen so many clan vehicles—why, all six lanes were blocked, hub to hub and bumper to bumper. Ahead, up and down the undulations of southern Kentucky, the jam went on and on; six lanes were lit up with headlamps for miles. The spectacle unnerved him. For the first time he felt the full, crushing significance of this race with the maniac who was showing him red tails at 110-plus up ahead. All at once Billy grew more frightened than he'd ever been in his life.

The fear held him a minute. Then he mastered it. At least to the point where he could begin to think of what he must do. The Twister felt unreal under and around him; his hands had only nominal control. The slightest obstruction—a bump; a blown tire—and he'd be through.

That didn't seem to bother Big Daddy. He was still pushing it way over 100 mph. Billy shoved his half-boot down, pushed the pedal against the floor and kept it there.

Now the lacy shuddering of the Twister became even more exquisite, as if the machine flowed on a ribbon of glass. But Big Daddy's tails began to grow larger again.

With his left hand Billy knuckled his blurry eyes. That didn't do any good. Big Daddy's red tails began to multiply, spots blinking red in the wrong place.

157

Then, squinching his eyes, Billy recognized the mis-placed light. The radiophone.

He held the Twister right at 94 mph while he fiddled. He picked up a snatch of the Fed band, finally zeroed on the intercar wavelength, yelled, "Who is this? What do you want?"

"Billy!" Repeated, the name punched through his anger. "It's Ferd Spoiler."

"Of all the dumb goddamn times to—"

"Billy, I hadda call you. Listen to me. One of the kids went down to the bay to find somethin' and—Billy, Rose Ann was down there."

Like ice: a memory. As he left tonight, above the mill's roar, someone calling his name. Thinking it imagination, he hadn't paid the slightest mind.

"What was Rose Ann doing down there, Ferd?"

"Billy, she's hurt. Like—somebody run over her. Billy —oh my God, I'm no doc but I think she's hurt some-thing terrible."

And then Billy remembered the shuddery impact that ran through the Twister as he backed out, wild with nerves and not thinking properly. He'd imagined that the bump was part of the racket and jarring when he missteered the machine up onto the edge of the ramp channel, then banged her down again in one incoherent moment.

Billy rubbed his throat. Up ahead, Big Daddy Hard-charger hit his brake lights, *flash,* off, *flash,* off, *flash.* Billy could feel the rage: *Come on, are you yellowing out?*

"Billy? You there?"

"I'm here, Ferd."

"I put the van on the strip and went down to take a look at her. Oh Billy, she's banged up awful, but she's awake. She wants to come up here and talk to you. She says she's gotta. She wants me to help her move but I wouldn't. I'm afraid she's all broke up—"

"Don't you let her move, Ferd, you hear what I say? Don't you dare let her move. I'll try to find a wheeldoc." And he snapped over to the Fed band, hollering for help, for anybody, till a voice broke in:

"This is traffic counselor Mountjoy with the Patrol. Who's this?"

"Road machine," Billy said. The call light began to blink again, indicating someone wanting to get in touch. "Listen, my wife's hurt real bad. She's in a road van about—well, where are you?"

"Near the Corbin off ramps, where are you?"

"Still north of there, but I don't think very far."

"You say you need medical assistance?"

"Yes, and goddamn fast. Listen, I'll call you back in a minute."

"We'll get on it," Mountjoy said, the last words disappearing down a drain of scratch as Billy dialed through, trying to locate the source of the call making the red light blink. His mind raced a blue streak. How would the wheeldoc—*if* they found one—pick them up? He glanced over at the jammed northbounds. Not a chance of getting through that way and looping back. The only chance was for the wheeldoc to pull onto the southbounds at Corbin, or the next ramps below.

Keeping the Twister steady at 87 mph with one hand, Billy finally located the source of the call: Big Daddy.

"What's with you, Spoiler-boy? You gonna yella out?"

"You can go grease yourself," Billy yelled. "My wife's hurt."

"Oh, don't give me none of that bullshit, boy. I can smell yella a mile off. Now you either put some balls 'tween your legs and catch up or everybody's gonna know—"

The tiny red light flashed. Billy howled an obscenity at Big Daddy and switched over: "Who is it?"

"This is Ferd again—" In the background—Billy's bowels tied up tight as a string—he heard her calling his name.

"Ferd, goddamn it, I told you—"

"I couldn't help it, Billy. She crawled up here all by herself—*Rose Ann, look out*—"

A tangle of bumping noises; static; a cry of pain. Ferd said, "Billy, she fell, just a second—oh God, Rose Ann, here, try to stretch out—"

More static. Then her voice, extremely loud. "Billy? Can you hear me?"

159

"I hear you. Rose Ann, don't cry. You're crying, Rose Ann—"

"Billy, be careful. The power steering's foxed."

Billy sat numb, both hands locked on the wheel, ignoring the flash-on, blink-off of the tiny red light; either Big Daddy or the Patrol calling in. He said, "Foxed? What do you mean foxed?"

"She's liable to go out on you. I sneaked over last night with Werty, he helped me fox it. He did most of it. The vans are never locked up tight; we got in all right—"

"You and Werty? Werty Ramp? Oh, Rose Ann, why?"

"Because you looked at me like stone! Because you acted like you didn't care any more! Not about anything! And—"

She sucked in air; moaned. He was dying from the hurt of listening.

"—I got so mad, I wanted to do *something* so you'd know I was alive—so you'd know I felt—oh, Billy. Oh my God, I'm sorry. I told Lee, he fixed it up with Werty— we did it."

"You went to Lee? You went to Lee last night?"

"Yes, I did, oh God I'm so sorry." She was beginning to sound completely out of her mind.

"Rose Ann, listen—"

"And tonight—oh, Billy, he threw me out. He threw me out right before he went off to pace you. I was drinking too much—I laughed at him—oh, Billy, I lied to you last night, I've never been with him since baby Rose Ann, never—like that, only to drink beers and kiss a little, that's all—oh, Billy, I lied, I lied—"

It poured out, a torrent; he could barely decipher separate words. The world dropped down through his belly to the bottom, pressing heavy and hurting.

"—he's crippled all the way, Billy, he can't do anything with a woman, not anything—oh, Billy, I laughed at him, he hit me—all of a sudden, I came to—oh, Billy sweetheart, oh my God maybe I'm low but I'm not that low—I didn't mean to ask them to fox the steering— that's what I came back to tell you tonight, so you wouldn't go race—I got in the van but you were backing out."

"Oh Jesus," Billy said, tears flowing. "Oh, Rose Ann

160

honey, oh my God." He tried to get hold of himself. "Ferd? Ferd!"

"Please, Billy, oh please forgive me—I don't want—oh God. Oh my God."

"Ferd?"

"I hear you, Billy."

"I'll get there. Don't let her talk any more."

"She can't, Billy. She passed out. You better hurry. She looks awful, she's doubled up."

"Put the draggers down." A monster sign loomed. "Corbin. I'm two miles from Corbin. I'll pull off. I'll wait till you catch up. I can't loop back, the northbounds are full."

Horror-stricken, Ferd's voice came through. "You mean you're goin' to get off and wait? You're goin' to stop?"

"You just put those god damn dragging ramps down, you hear me?"

He kicked the voice off with the butt of one palm. He grabbed the wheel tight with both hands, booted her over to the next right lane, then the next. The tiny red dashlight continued to flash. Far ahead, Big Daddy's red tails were still visible.

Billy concentrated all his attention on the job of maneuvering toward the exit lane that opened on the right. He fought with the steering; he had to pull and haul on the wheel; but now he understood why.

A clan van came on, riding the extreme right lane. Billy horned it back, straightened the Twister, driving like fury. A great sparkly-green arrow pointed him to the exit.

Billy dropped the Twister's speed. Below, to the left and right of the elevated super, Corbin glistened behind the mixed rain and snow. He slid onto the ramp, angling down and curving around right. The red dashlight continued to blink.

He thought he spotted a stars-and-stripes turbine way below him, at the bottom of the giant right-running bend. He fished for the correct band, in case it was the Federal Highway Patrol signaling. It was:

"—the Road plate that wanted a mobile doctor?"

"Yeh, that's me. Where are you?"

161

"Parked in the service space at the bottom of the Corbin off ramp."

"I see you. I see your lights." But he saw four sets. He ground his knuckles into his eyes. "How many are you?"

A new, familiar voice crackled on: "This is traffic counselor Mountjoy. The officers are in a different car. Where are you?"

"Coming down the ramp."

The first voice; sterner; alarmed: "Those your lights we see? That you?"

"Yeh, right, where's the wheeldoc?"

Mountjoy cleared his throat. "I've been trying, I've been radiophoning all over. With this weather—"

Holding even down the ramp at 55 mph, Billy hollered, "Where's the doc?"

"The nearest we can find is circling down by Knoxville."

"That's an hour!" Billy screamed back. "That's maybe two hours! Listen, my wife's in one of the road vans, didn't you get me? She's hurt! She needs help right now, not two hours from now." He whipped his hands over his pants, first one palm, then the other, to rid himself of the sweat that came through his pores like oil. He thought through the blindness of his suddenly-killing sinus and his fear. Then: "Okay, all right. I'll stop in Corbin. I'll pick up a doc from a hosp or—"

"We could try to pick up one for you," Mountjoy said. "Maybe deliver him—"

"Try?" Spittle-mouthed, Billy told them what they could do with that suggestion. "How long you been trying already? Screwing around! Rose Ann's dying, maybe. *Dying!*"

The voice of the Special Officer cracked, "We're watching your lights coming down. You're coming too fast."

Mountjoy cleared his throat, a man of weak but not unkindly voice: "Garringer? Might be better if we made an exception and let him—"

"No exception," said the officer.

Billy let off on the gas pedal; the Twister began to slacken speed.

He felt the rear sway lessen. The roadbed became more like concrete, less like glass. He was perhaps halfway

162

down the ramp; halfway to the point where the double sets of lights gleamed through the slash of the storm. The officer finished up:

"The law's the law, Mountjoy. Knoxville will have to be it. Listen, Road plate, we're not trying to make it tough, but—"

"I'm stopping," Billy broke in. "I'm getting off."

Someone with Garringer—his co-Patrolman?—said something in a warning tone; what, Billy couldn't hear. The tiny red light blinked. He switched over. Ferd's voice.

"Billy, she's twisting around something awful. You better hurry."

"I'm picking up a doc at Corbin. I'll catch up."

Just the faint beginning of a little throat-catch of horror rattled over the band before Billy snapped off. Through the beating of his wipers shoving hardening slush aside, he saw the first set of headlamps below begin to move. He didn't understand for a second or so. Then he heard the traffic counselor:

"Garringer, are you sure you want to?"

"Hurt wife or no hurt wife, he's not stopping. That's the law."

"Whose law?" Billy shouted; but he bit it off instantly when the situation cleared itself through to his mind.

He dropped to about 47 mph, scrubbed his eyes to rid them of the sweat that kept accumulating there; watched the headlamps nosing forward down below. The Federal Highway Patrol turbine was pulling from the service space, angling across the double lane to block him.

Shadows flitted through the headlamp glow. Men, a pair of them. They were out in front of their vehicle. Blocking him.

"This is Mountjoy, Road plate. Can you see what's happened?"

"Tell those bastards to get out of the way."

"They want you to bear left at the crossover, Road plate. They've got you blocked; you can't get off. Listen, you're almost to the cross."

The Twister went by it, a left-shooting horizontal that traveled straight south to intersect the on ramp rising from below. The shadow-figures waved. One's right hand suddenly burst into light. A flare—

They thought they could stop him. Well, they'd learn different. He kept boring in at a steady 45 mph, maybe a half mile from them now. In another second, they'd jump back into their flashy turbine, squeal it into reverse. They'd see he meant business.

"You better not try to go by them, Road plate," Mountjoy warned. "You better brake her. Illegal stopping is better than causing a wreck."

"Tell them to get out of the way or I'll kill them."

"You damn fool," Mountjoy exclaimed, "they already radiophoned for more cars. Two or three are coming out from the Corbin post right now."

"Tell them to get out of the way."

"Listen, you crazy pophead, don't try to bluff—"

"My wife's *hurt!*"

"But the government doesn't allow stopping of Road cars for any—"

The rest he failed to hear; terror clogged him from his belly to his head. He was committed, hurtling at 45 mph.

A quarter of a mile from the turbine.

An eighth of a mile.

The downslope accelerated him. The Special Officer waved the flare so fast that it became a pink half-circle. They weren't going to move! They weren't going to pull the machine out of the way!

At the last second the Patrol officers jumped. But he was still going to hit the turbine.

Full of fear, Billy yanked the wheel left, aiming to shoot up and over the low median to the up ramp, missing them if possible. He gripped the wheel so hard his fingers hurt.

The right front corner of the Twister smacked the turbine, sent it hurtling backward. Billy's front tires slammed the median. The hood lifted.

He crashed up, over, down the other side, hurtling at the guardrail. He tore the wheel right again, fishtailed, breathing in noisy, moaning gulps. Sleet and lights blurred sidewise in his vision as he struggled to pull her out, *pull her out.*

He caromed off the guardrail, spun back toward the

164

median, hauled left on the wheel, straightened, went slipping and skidding down the up ramp and hit the flat in a merging circle at the bottom.

Headlamps bored at him along a feeder road that entered the circle on the far side. A flash began to whip bars of red light through the snowy darkness. A second flash started up on the turbine right behind. Patrol. Coming head on! He kicked the Twister into a maniacal slide.

He brought her all the way around, heeling up on her left tires, the whole frame shaking. Then he crashed down and beat the living hell out of the gas pedal.

The mother's frame vibrated. He heard the two Patrol howlers going full blast. He was running in panic now, giving her all she had, barreling up the on ramp to escape the pursuit. Headlamps blazed briefly on the left. Mountjoy; starting up.

He said all the obscene things he'd ever heard, said them to the Patrol right over the open band. He was shaking and weeping. Yet he was maneuvering the old Twister well, in spite of the power steering. He checked the rearvision.

Three cars were riding him. But he was outdistancing them, slamming up the on ramp at 55 mph; 60 mph; pouring it on.

The turbines with flashes operating were the second and third machines. For some reason the traffic counselor had decided to chase him, too. Well, shaft them all; he'd find help at the next exit.

He roared onto the slick multilane, horning out between two clan vans, sliding left into a clear stretch. He gave the Twister plenty. She responded, though shakily. In less than three minutes, he caught up with Uncle Sammy's service van.

The rear doors were open. The dragging ramps were down. Lights shone in the bay. Billy pulled even with the ramps and held there while he called Ferd. The report wasn't good. "She ain't moved, Billy. She's breathing, but pretty light. She really needs help. Once in a while she lets out a moan like—" He couldn't continue.

"I'll find a doc at the next exit," Billy told him.

"Couldn't get off at the last one. The goddamn Patrol—never mind. You hang on. I'll be back."

And he accelerated up past the head of the van.

He checked his rear again. He saw Patrol flashes back there, vivid red. But they were still behind another set of lamps that must belong to the traffic counselor's machine. The radiophone blinked.

The Twister began to skim and slide again as he picked up speed. He snapped on the radiophone, hearing Mountjoy call him.

"What do you want?" Billy yelled.

"I'm holding the Patrol back. They want to pick you up."

"Let them try. This old mother can take three of them."

"You'll be in real trouble if you try to pull off at the next exit, Road plate. My job's to counsel some sense into you."

"Sense! You're crazy. You're wobbly in the head. My wife's—"

"Road plate, I understand that. But Federal law prohibits stopping."

"I heard that before," Billy sneered. "We don't make these here laws, we're just doing our job. Trying to kill my wife, that's your job. Listen, I'm going to stop at the next off ramp and I don't care who gets hurt."

"But you'll never make it, Road plate. The blocks are already up."

About to scream again, Billy didn't. Shocks were coming too fast. He sucked air, noisily. Mountjoy kept talking, trying to soothe, to reason. "You're lucky neither one of those Special Officers was injured back at Corbin. Now if you'll just throttle off and let us take over—"

"I'm stopping."

"It's a Federal crime if you do."

"Bullshit. It's just road ways—never let the old speed fall—"

"It started out that way, maybe," Mountjoy agreed. "But it isn't that way any longer. I'll let you in on something if that's the only way I can talk sense into you."

Right then Billy's head began to buzz. He didn't want to listen; Mountjoy was trying to hypnotize him; talking to

166

him across the intercar band to keep him busy, keep him occupied and doing no more damage. He started to show Mountjoy his tails. But he didn't put his boot all the way down. Something in him wanted the truth; all the truth of what he'd suspected but the others—Colonel Tal, all the others—denied in their fright. He heard Mountjoy:

"—four or five years ago, the Federal government started enforcing what began as a Road custom—never let you Road people off the superhighways; never let you travel below forty; never let you stop—Road plate? Are you there?"

"I hear you. I don't believe you." But he really did.

"See, it makes sense, though, doesn't it? I mean, you can understand—why else would the Federal government issue special Road plates? And put all you people on the dole? Things got so bad—are you still there?"

Transfixed, Billy stared at the radiophone. "Yeh."

"The only answer was, keep you Road clans moving on the road."

Billy said, "Why?"

"Too many people."

"What?"

"Too many people in the U.S. You've been on the supers on weekends—you've seen the cars, haven't you? Too many people. If you think that's bad, you should see the cities. Jammed. Jammed to the breaking point. Nobody lives out in the country any more. The country's a wasteland; it became a problem about ten years ago. Everyone was in the cities, and the cities were breaking down. Ten years ago—that was right before I took my traffic counselor examination; right after my wife and I got married. Listen, Road plate, you've got to understand —I feel for you. I'm just laying it out so you won't cause any more trouble. You'll just get in a worse fix if you do."

"What happened ten years ago?"

"The Federal computers found out that nobody was living in the country anymore. They were all in the cities; the country wouldn't even support life any longer; it had just fallen to waste. Then the Federal computers pumped out the fact that the country's urbanized—I mean the city population—was reaching critical stage. The government

167

had to do something because people wouldn't stop having children and Congress was still afraid to do anything about *that*—well, for the general public, I mean. They passed a couple of token laws for Federal employees. When I started as a traffic counselor, my wife and I had to pledge no more than one child. Instead of passing laws for the public, the government started all sorts of programs. Climate domes in Alaska. Encouraging businessmen, creative types to live in other countries; give them a tax break if they did. Bonuses if people moved out of the megs and tried to homestead on farms. With the country deserted—wild in a lot of places; wolves, even—well, that scheme didn't work either. Another of the ideas was keep the Road clans where they were. Since the clans were already living on the highways, the government decided not to let them off. If the clans ever moved *en masse* from the roads to the cities, that would add another ten percent to the population right away."

Special plates; special dole; the memory of Reverend Cleatus Cloverleaf saying that some outsiders claimed the country was too crowded, but they were liars—it all buzzed and whined through Billy's head in a horrible pudding of confusion. He would have scoffed except for one thing he remembered: the way the Special Officers had given up so easily, the first time they searched for his i.c. underhood mother. They were pretending to hunt for an illegal machine; but they didn't search very hard; they really wanted him to stay on the road, illegal machine or no illegal machine.

"You don't know how bad it is, Road plate," Mountjoy kept on. "The whole country's moving these days—one meg to another—why, you ought to see the psych reports of the guys who work in Traffic Central. Crackups every week. Every day! That's why it's so important that you Road people stay on the highways. You're ten percent of the whole population. If you were down below in the megs with the stoppers, it might all stop—I mean, everything— everything in the megs—bang, just like that."

Billy held the Twister steady. Checked rearward again. The Patrol flashes remained about in the position they'd

168

held earlier: a mile, mile and a half back, with another vehicle leading—Mountjoy.

Billy felt drained; whipped. But he managed to hold the old, groaning machine on a straight course through the slashing wet of the superhighway. He passed vans full of spectators. He kept his head averted slightly to the right to avoid the glare of the nonstop traffic on the north-bounds. The radiophone's tiny red eye began to wink. Ferd? Big Daddy? Weak, he listened to Mountjoy's drone:

"Beginning to understand, Road plate? I shouldn't admit all this to you, but I know you're in a bad personal situation, and I'm trying to help. The only way I can help is to keep you from causing more trouble, and the only way I can keep you from that is by explaining—"

"How come road folks never find out?"

"One in ten thousand does, Road plate. In emergencies like this. I won't even tell you what penalty the Federal government puts on it if you tell anyone else and the word gets back."

Billy sighed. "Hell—the folks wouldn't believe it."

"Yes, but do you?"

Billy's answer was, "I tried stopping already. The clan folks never did. Hey—"

"What's that, Road plate?"

"You said you worked for the government?"

"Yes, right."

"You work for General Ford Motors Company."

"General Ford Motors Company is the government."

Thickness inside Billy's windpipe: "Come again?"

"Right after the two biggest auto companies merged into one—that was probably before you were born; they drove the third one out of business—the government took it over. Quietly. Most stoppers in high government positions know it. The fact's never publicized, that's all. Actually, the factories are run no differently than they have been for the last thirty years—computerized assembly, everything self-repairing—"

Billy scratched the back of his neck. "No people?"

"Not many. Supervisors of the equipment. Managers of marketing, output—"

"Why'd the government take it over?"

169

"Because it had become too big and important an industry to be left in private hands. Too many jobs were tied up—too much went wrong in the economy when there were strikes—oh, a lot of reasons."

"Country's so damn clogged up like you say, too many machines and all, and General Ford Motors Company keeps sludging out the new ones? Doesn't make sense."

"Well, it got out of hand, Road plate."

"What did?"

"How much the auto came to mean to the country—all out of hand, too fast. Like I said—too many people dependent on the industry for jobs. Too much meg construction geared to wheel travel. The government caught up to it too late, that's all. I don't want to get into a lot of economics but I guarantee you, Road plate, if General Ford Motors ever shut down, so would the nation."

Billy said nothing. After a pause, Mountjoy went on, "Believe me, Road plate, I feel for your situation. We're trying to locate a doctor and wheel him up here."

"If he's coming from Knoxville he'll never get through on those northbounds," Billy responded in a dull voice. He felt beaten; saturated with too much he didn't want to know. He glanced over to the right, out past the rail at the rim of the superhighway. Down below in the dark and snow, he glimpsed mile on mile of lights. *Swollen fat,* his mind kept saying to him. *Swollen all fat.*

"Then there's the immense amount of economic product General Ford Motors generates in the form of materiel for the Oriental war. I hear the figure is way up in the—"

"I don't want to hear any more," Billy said.

"What? What's that?"

"I said, I heard enough." Billy stared down the light-tunnels. Far ahead, he saw red tails. On the road. On the move. Forever. Forever.

"Road plate?"

"What?"

Mountjoy sounded weary. "Now you understand why the Patrol can't let you stop? Probably each and every one of them—personally—I mean, if it was up to them—they would. But when laws are set up by the government, and the whole thing's in such a close, tricky balance, you can appreciate what would happen if another ten percent of the population was spilled back into the megs. You can appreciate that, can't you? You sound a smarter than average—"

"Oh," said Billy with a jerk of his mouth, "yeh. I get it."

"The Patrol officers aren't monsters, they're not—"

"Just doing their jobs," Billy finished, so tired he could just barely see. The radiophone kept up its *wink*-black, *wink*-black, until he had an urge to tear it out of its mounting.

"Feel bad about it myself," Mountjoy told him. "It's as if we're all caught up in one big machine that's gone wild. People used to talk about autos setting us free. Maybe they did. But somewhere along the line, we lost that. But the factories kept running. I don't know how to stop it; nobody knows how to stop it."

"And is escairt to try," Billy said. When Mountjoy asked for a repeat, he said, "Never mind."

Oh, Jesus. Oh, merciful Savior, he was weary. He felt like no one had ever been so alone, either, moving it near 70 mph down the unrolling concrete that went on, and went on, through rain, through sunshine, through Kansas, through Connecticut, through birth, through school, through kissing, through screwing, through stepping around, through death—through and on, through and on; the monster snowpelted night ahead was created to swallow and swallow and keep swallowing him, his lifetime, forever and ever. But no amen.

"I told you all this so you'd understand," Mountjoy repeated. "So you wouldn't get yourself in worse trouble."

Billy said, "Yeh."

"I've got the Patrol band damped out, you understand. They can't hear. I hope you feel better about—"

"No," Billy said. Then a shout: "No! I wish you hadn't said a thing. I wish you'd kept your goddamn mouth shut!"

And he slapped off, broke the connection, bam, hard.

He sat just idling her along, one hand on the touchy wheel. With his other hand he tried to compress the pain between his eyeballs. It didn't work. When he looked again, the radiophone light was still going on and off.

He dialed in. "It's Ferd. Where you been?"

"Here, Ferd. What is it?"

"Billy, she—Billy—"

"Tell me." Silence. "I already know. She's dead."

"Billy, I wish—"

He reached out and killed the hollow, sad voice and sat staring up the tunnel of highway to forever and forever more.

"But no amen," he said aloud. Then he thought, *I must be going crazy.*

He reached over and closed his hand over his upper left arm and held on tight. He smelled lilac.

Then he began to weep, but without sound, the only visible sign the tracks of wet down his cheeks.

The windshield wipers kept knocking ridges of slush aside. He stared at the red tails a mile or two ahead. Then, with loud breathing, he dialed, dialing on by Mountjoy, catching just a scratch of him:—"Patrol's asking whether you'll back off—"

Dialing, hunting, Billy said, "Big Daddy? Big Daddy?"

"Where you been, you little chickenturd?"

"I think I see you. That you up ahead of me?"

The red tails brightened, died back to normal, and did it a second time.

"Yeh," Billy said, "I see you."

"An' I see a couple of big red flashes chasin' you, boy. What kind of stuff are you pullin'?"

"Don't worry about the Patrol. I didn't call them."

"Well, you listen. I'm tired of tiddlin' with myself and waiting to find out whether—"

"You shut your fucking mouth and just drive," Billy said, kicking off the band, shoving his halfboot onto the gas pedal and giving her everything, all she could stand and more.

The Twister shivered. The power steering plant gave of another of those gravely squeals. The roadway began to be a thing of less and less substance beneath the yammering belts.

No more tears ran down Billy's cheeks. Everything inside him had shut down, gone off, snap. His head was filled with great empty silence. His cold bones rode easy inside his numb skin.

172

He felt easier, more comfortable, than he had all night. It was a comfort compounded of silence and total absence of feeling. With one exception, nothing seemed quite real: not the unending chains of lights in the northbounds, coming on and coming on, to gawk, watch, applaud; not the double whip of red light from the Patrol turbines swinging out around the traffic counselor's machine and howling their right-of-way; not the truth of what Mountjoy had told him. Billy tried to imagine Mountjoy: a man of white pallor; of earnest softness; a man who'd never heard the wind scream over the bubble of an underhood i.c. mill and never would; a poor little white worm whom Billy was not convinced really existed.

The single reality on which everything focused was the rear deck of Big Daddy Hardcharger's low, chopped machine—there came the monsters in view; there came the flames; there the orgiastic painted ladies, as Billy slid up from behind on the right, hitting 92 mph, 93 mph.

Up past the rear wheel well.

Then drawn even, hub to hub.

Big Daddy yanked her over, a careless, clumsy, too-hard motion without style; it telegraphed his plans.

The noise of Big Daddy's mill beat like thunder through the glass on Billy's side. Big Daddy's machine seemed to float, to drift, slowly—as everything did—till Billy wrenched motion back into the world: wrenched his wheel right, fishtailing his rear end across to crash Big Daddy before Big Daddy could crash him.

Something in the Twister crumpled and squealed under the hood; a loud, distinct pop.

Billy's jawbone transmitted the shock to his clenched teeth as he whipped back out of the crash, then wrenched the wheel again, snapping his front end over to hit Big Daddy before he'd had a chance to recover from the first blow. Billy crashed with full fury, full speed.

His hands were frozen on the wheel; skin become plasto; plasto become skin. His left eye must be cut; he was blind; he didn't feel the blood; he hadn't heard the ragged glass of his left window shatter. He heard the wind but did not feel it. He gave everything to one huge left-swiping crash, taking Big Daddy's skating machine broad-

173

side, crash, full into the side with an impact that spanged Billy's Twister off like a ball off a billiard cushion, sent him angling ahead and away, rightward, floating, turning, rotating into a spin.

He hung onto the wheel trying to pull her out straight. But the grindings and poppings under the hood grew louder. Suddenly he smelled smoke beyond the firewall, and all control was gone.

The Twister revolved in a complete circle, then started around again as it spun toward the right hand edge of the elevated highway.

Lights began to streak out horizontally as he came around. Yet one thing was etched clear: Big Daddy's machine dropping behind, wobbling low on its right front end, metal crashed, rubber cut, smoke beginning to billow from beneath the hood. Suddenly the entire front end dropped. Sparks gushed. Flames burst out from beneath the hood, burned through the firewall, filled the driver's compartment while the machine skidded along on its nose, wobbling but still in one lane, still hurtling 100 mph while real flames ate the painted ones, moving backward to the tank, the explosion, the fireball.

Billy's Twister drifted on around. Tears began to run down his cheeks again, tracks of them, terrible pouring relief.

The Twister spun into the right hand guardrail, crumpled it outward, broke it and let Billy go free into space inside his machine.

He rode upward through the dark, a dreamy-soft, elegant float beyond all pain. Up higher, up higher—

He wept and held the wheel that was part of him. He felt, finally, free; a strange, cool, not unpleasant thought tickled his mind. Now he would know what it felt like to stop.

On the way down he saw the Firebird.